**Harlequin Romance is excited to present
this new family saga from award-winning
author Lucy Gordon!**

The Falcon Dynasty
Five successful brothers looking for brides!

Amos Falcon is a proud, self-made man who wants
his legacy to live on through his five sons. Each son is
different, for they have different mothers, but in one
aspect they are the same: Amos has raised them to be
ruthless in business and sensible in matters of the heart.

One by one, these high-achieving brothers will find that
when the right woman comes along, love is the greatest
power of them all....

This month, read Darius Falcon's story in
Rescued by the Brooding Tycoon

Look for more heart-racing romances in this new series
by Lucy Gordon,
coming soon!

Dear Reader,

Years ago, "family" suggested a gathering of relatives living in or near the same place, certainly the same country. But as travel speeded up, the world grew smaller, and a family could be spread over great distances.

This has been useful to Amos Falcon, a man who believes in doing what suits himself. Starting poor, he pursued his dream of wealth through many countries, fathering sons in England, America, France and Russia.

In his eyes they were all his property. With a great fortune to distribute in his will, he studied them, wanting to see in each one a reflection of himself.

In a sense he found this. They all had their father's determination, skill, money-making ability and, when necessary, ruthlessness. But they also had qualities their father lacked. Some were gentle or generous, some had charm and each of them was waiting for the woman who could bring out his true nature.

Darius, the eldest, seemed most like his forbidding father, but his startling encounter with Harriet, an impudent young woman, turned his world upside down. Unlike most people, she wasn't afraid of him, and when she saved his life, it was the harbinger of another rescue—when she would save his heart and soul, and keep him safe forever.

On their wedding day, Darius's brothers gathered, knowing that if they, too, were lucky, the same day would dawn for them. Their stories have yet to be told.

I don't think I've ever liked one of my own heroines better than Harriet. Right to the end I was cheering her on, hoping that Darius would turn out to be good enough for her. But she thinks he is, and that's what really matters.

Lucy

LUCY GORDON

Rescued by the Brooding Tycoon

Harlequin®

TORONTO NEW YORK LONDON
AMSTERDAM PARIS SYDNEY HAMBURG
STOCKHOLM ATHENS TOKYO MILAN MADRID
PRAGUE WARSAW BUDAPEST AUCKLAND

Recycling programs
for this product may
not exist in your area.

ISBN-13: 978-0-373-17754-7

RESCUED BY THE BROODING TYCOON

First North American Publication 2011

Copyright © 2011 by Lucy Gordon

Lucy Gordon cut her writing teeth on magazine journalism, interviewing many of the world's most interesting men, including Warren Beatty, Charlton Heston and Roger Moore. She also camped out with lions in Africa, and had many other unusual experiences that have often provided the background for her books. Several years ago, while staying in Venice, she met a Venetian who proposed in two days. They have been married ever since. Naturally this has affected her writing, in which romantic Italian men tend to feature strongly.

Two of her books have won the Romance Writers of America RITA® Award.

You can visit her website at www.lucy-gordon.com.

I should like to dedicate this book to the
Royal National Lifeboat Institution,
without whose help my heroine could never have
been as spunky as she is.

CHAPTER ONE

IT WAS the burst of beauty that caught Darius unaware. He didn't regard himself as a man vulnerable to beauty. Efficiency, ruthlessness, financial acumen, these things could be counted on.

He'd been driven to hire a helicopter on the English mainland and fly five miles across the sea to the little island of Herringdean. Since it was now his property, it made good sense to inspect it briefly on his way to an even more important meeting.

Good sense. Cling to that, since everything else had failed him.

But the sudden vision of sunlit sea, the waves glittering as they broke against the sand, stunned him and made him press closer to the window.

'Go lower,' he commanded, and watched as the helicopter descended, sweeping along the coast of Herringdean Island. From here he could study the place with a critical eye.

Or so he believed. But there was no criticism in the glance he turned on the lush green cliffs, the golden beaches; only astonished pleasure.

The cliffs were sinking until they were only a few feet higher than the beach. He could see a large house that must once have been elegant, but was now fast falling into disrepair. In front of it stretched a garden leading to a plain lawn, close to the sand.

In the far distance were buildings that must be Ellarick, the largest town on the island: population twenty thousand.

'Land here,' he said, 'on that lawn.'

'I thought you wanted to fly over the town,' the pilot protested.

But suddenly he yearned to avoid towns, cars, crowds. The beach seemed to call to him. It was an unfamiliar sensation for a man who wasn't normally impulsive. In the financial world impulsiveness could be dangerous, yet now he yielded with pleasure to the need to explore below.

'Go lower,' he repeated urgently.

Slowly the machine sank onto the lawn. Darius leapt out, a lithe figure whose fitness and agility belied the desk-bound businessman he usually was, and hurried down to the beach. The sand was slightly damp, but smooth and hard, presenting little threat to his expensive appearance.

That appearance had been carefully calculated to inform the world that here was a successful man who could afford to pay top prices for his clothes. A few grains of sand might linger on his handmade shoes but they could be easily brushed off, and it was a small price to pay for what the beach offered him.

Peace.

After the devastating events that had buffeted him recently there was nothing more blessed than to stand here in the sunlight, throw his head back, close his eyes, feel the soft breeze on his face, and relish the silence.

So many years spent fighting, conspiring, manoeuvring, while all the time this simple perfection had been waiting, and he hadn't realised.

Outwardly, Darius seemed too young for such thoughts;

in his mid-thirties, tall, strong, attractive, ready to take on the world. Inwardly, he knew otherwise. He had already taken on the world, won some battles, lost others, and was weary to his depths.

But here there could be a chance to regain strength for the struggles that lay ahead. He breathed in slowly, yielding himself to the quiet, longing for it to last.

Then it ended.

A shriek of laughter tore the silence, destroying the peace. With a groan he opened his eyes and saw two figures in the sea, heading for the shore. As they emerged from the water he realised that one of them was a large dog. The other was a young woman in her late twenties with a lean, athletic build, not voluptuous but dashingly slender, with long elegant legs. Her costume was a modest black one-piece, functional rather than enticing, and her brown hair was pinned severely back out of the way.

As a man much pursued by women, Darius knew they commonly used swimming as a chance to parade their beauty. But if this girl was sending out any message to men it was, *I wear what's useful, so don't kid yourself that I'm flaunting my body to attract you.*

'Can I help you?' she cried merrily as she bounced up the beach.

'I'm just looking round, getting the feel of the place.'

'Yes, it's wonderful, isn't it? Sometimes I think if I ever get to heaven it'll be just like this. Not that I expect to go to heaven. They slam the gates on characters like me.'

Although he would have died before admitting it, the reference to heaven so exactly echoed his own thoughts that now he found he could forgive her for interrupting him.

'Characters like what?' he asked.

'Awkward,' she said cheerfully. 'Lots of other things too, but chiefly awkward. That's what my friends say.'

'Those friends who haven't been driven away by your awkwardness?'

'Right.'

He indicated the house behind him. 'I believe that belongs to Morgan Rancing.'

'Yes, but if you've come to see him you've had a wasted journey. Nobody knows where he is.'

Rancing was on the far side of the world, hiding from his creditors, including himself, but Darius saw no need to mention that.

She stepped back to survey him, a curious look in her eyes. Then it vanished as though an idea had occurred to her, only to be dismissed as impossible.

'You're lucky Rancing isn't here,' she observed. 'He'd hit the roof at you bringing down your machine on his land. Nobody's allowed on his property.'

'Does that include this beach?' he asked, regarding the fences that enclosed the stretch of sand.

'It certainly does.' She gave a chuckle. 'Be a sport. If you see him, don't say you caught me on his private beach. He disapproves of my swimming here.'

'But you do it anyway,' he observed wryly.

'It's so lovely that I can't resist. The other beaches are full of holidaymakers but here you can have it all to yourself; just you and the sun and the sky.' She flung out her arms in a dramatic gesture, smiling up at him. 'The world is yours.'

Darius nodded, feeling a curious sense of ease at the way her thoughts chimed with his own, and looked at her with renewed interest. Despite her boyish air, she wasn't lacking in feminine charm. There was real beauty in her eyes, that were large and deep blue, full of life, seeming to invite him into a teasing conspiracy.

'That's very true,' he said.

'So you won't tell him that you saw me on his private beach?'

'Actually, it's my private beach.'

Her smile vanished. 'What do you mean?'

'This island is mine now.'

'Rancing sold it to you?' she gasped.

Without knowing it, she'd said the fatal word. Rancing hadn't sold him the island, he'd tricked him into it. In a flash, his goodwill towards her vanished, and a stubborn expression overtook his face. 'I told you it's mine,' he said harshly. 'That's all that matters. My name is Darius Falcon.'

She drew a quick breath. 'I thought I'd seen your face before, in the newspaper. Weren't you the guy who—?'

'Never mind that,' he interrupted curtly. He knew his life, both private and business, had been all over the papers, and he didn't like being reminded of it. 'Perhaps now you'll tell me who you are.'

'Harriet Connor,' she said. 'I have an antique shop in Ellarick.'

'I shouldn't think you get much trade in this place,' he said, looking around at the isolation.

'On the contrary, Herringdean attracts a lot of tourists. Surely you knew that?'

The question, *How could you buy it without knowing about it?* hung in the air. Since he wasn't prepared to discuss the ignominious way he'd been fooled, he merely shrugged.

From behind Harriet came a loud yelp. The dog was charging up the beach, spraying water everywhere, heading straight for Darius.

'Steady, Phantom,' she called, trying to block his way.

'Keep him off me,' Darius snapped.

But it was too late. Gleeful at the sight of a stranger to

investigate, the dog hurled himself the last few feet, reared up on his hind legs and slammed his wet, sandy paws down on Darius's shoulders. He was a mighty beast, able to meet a tall man face to face, and lick him enthusiastically.

'Get him off me. He's soaking.'

'Phantom, get down!' Harriet cried.

He did so but only briefly, hurling himself at Darius again, this time with a force that took them both down to the ground. As he lay helplessly on the sand, Phantom loomed over him, licking his face and generally trying to show friendliness. He looked aggrieved as his mistress hauled him off.

'Bad dog! I'm very cross with you.'

Darius got to his feet, cursing at the wreck of his suit.

'He wasn't attacking you,' Harriet said in a pleading voice. 'He just likes people.'

'Whatever his intentions, he's made a mess,' Darius said in an icy voice.

'I'll pay to have your suit cleaned.'

'Cleaned?' he snapped. 'I'll send you a bill for a new one. Keep away from me, you crazy animal.'

He put up his arm to ward off another encounter, but Harriet threw her arms protectively around the dog.

'You'd better go,' she said in a voice that was now as icy as his own. 'I can't hold him for ever.'

'You should know better than to let a creature that size run free.'

'And you should know better than to wear a suit like that on the beach,' she cried.

The undeniable truth of this soured his temper further, leaving him no choice but to storm off in the direction of the helicopter. He guessed his pilot had seen everything, but the man was too wise to comment.

As they lifted off, Darius looked down and saw Harriet

gazing at the machine, one hand shielding her eyes. Then Phantom reared up again, enclosing her in his great paws, and at once she forgot the helicopter to cuddle the dog, while he licked her face. So much for being cross with that stupid mutt, Darius thought furiously. Clearly, he was all she cared about.

He thought of how he'd stood on the beach, alone, peaceful for the first time in months, and how clumsily she had destroyed that moment. He wouldn't forgive her for that.

From this high point on the hill overlooking Monte Carlo, Amos Falcon could see the bay but, unlike his son, he failed to notice the beauty of the sea. His attention was all for the buildings on the slope, tall, magnificent, speaking of money, though none spoke so loudly as his own house, a sprawling, three-storey edifice, bought because it dominated its surroundings.

It was money and the need to protect it that had first brought him to this tax haven years ago. He'd started life poor in a rundown mining town in the north of England, and got out fast. Working night and day, he'd built up a fortune of his own, helped by marrying a woman with wealth, and he'd left England for a more friendly tax regimen as soon as he could, determined that no government would be allowed to rob him of his gains.

'Where the devil is he?' he muttered crossly. 'It's not like Darius to be late. He knows I want him here before the others.'

Janine, his third wife, a well-preserved woman in her fifties with a kind face and a gentle manner, laid a hand on his arm.

'He's a busy man,' she said. 'His company is in trouble—'

'Everyone's company is in trouble,' Amos growled. 'He should be able to deal with it. I've taught him well.'

'Perhaps you spent too much time teaching him,' she suggested. 'He's your son, not just a business associate to be instructed.'

'He's no business associate of mine,' Amos said. 'I said I'd taught him well, but he never quite learned how to take the final, necessary step.'

'Because he has a conscience,' she suggested. 'He can be ruthless, but only up to a point.'

'Exactly. I could never quite make him see… Ah, well, maybe his recent troubles will have taught him a lesson.'

'You mean his wife leaving him?'

'I mean that damn fool divorce settlement he gave her. Much too generous. He just let her have whatever she demanded.'

Janine sighed. She'd heard him ranting on this subject so often, and there was no end to it.

'He did it for the children's sake,' she pointed out.

'He could have got his children back if he'd played hard, but he wouldn't do it.'

'Good for him,' Janine murmured.

Amos scowled. He could forgive her sentimental view of life. After all, she was a woman. But sometimes it exasperated him.

'That's all very well,' he growled, 'but then the world imploded.'

'Only the financial world,' she ventured.

His caustic look questioned whether there was any other kind, but he didn't rise to the bait.

'And suddenly he had a pittance compared to what he'd had before,' he continued. 'So he had to go back to that woman and try to persuade her to accept less. Naturally, she refused, and since the money had already been transferred to her he couldn't touch it.'

'You'd never have made that mistake,' Janine observed

wryly, perhaps thinking of the pre-nuptial agreement she'd had to sign before their wedding five years earlier. 'Never give anything you can't take back, that's your motto.'

'I never said that.'

'No, you've never actually said it,' she agreed quietly.

'Where the devil is he?'

'Don't upset yourself,' she pleaded. 'It's bad for you to get agitated after your heart attack.'

'I'm over that,' he growled.

'Until the next time. And don't say there won't be a next time because the doctor said a massive attack like that is always a warning.'

'I'm not an invalid,' he said firmly. 'Look at me. Do I look frail?'

He rose and stood against the backdrop of the sky, challenging her with his pose and his expression, and she had to concede the point. Amos was a big man, over six foot, broad-shouldered and heavy. All his life he'd been fiercely attractive, luring any woman he wanted, moving from marriage to affairs and on to marriage as the mood took him. Along the way, he'd fathered five sons by four mothers in different countries, thus spreading his tentacles across the world.

Recently, there had been an unexpected family reunion. Struck down by a heart attack, he'd lain close to death while his sons gathered at his bedside. But, against all the odds, he'd survived, and at last they had returned to their different countries.

Now he had summoned them back for a reason. Amos was making plans for the future. He'd regained much of his strength, although less than he claimed.

To the casual eye, he was a fine, healthy specimen, still handsome beneath a head of thick white hair. Only two people knew of the breathless attacks that followed exertion. One of them was Janine, his wife, who regarded him with a mixture of love and exasperation.

The other was Freya, Janine's daughter by an earlier marriage. A trained nurse, she'd recently come to stay at her mother's request.

'He doesn't want a nurse there in case it makes him look weak,' Janine pleaded, 'but if I invite my daughter he can't refuse.'

'But he knows I'm a nurse,' Freya had pointed out.

'Yes, but we don't have to talk about it, and you can keep an eye on him discreetly. It helps that you don't look like a nurse.'

This was an understatement. Freya was delicately built with elegant movements, a pretty face and a cheeky demeanour. She might have been a dancer, a nightclub hostess, or anything except a medical expert with an impressive list of letters after her name.

An adventurous spirit had made her leave her last job in response to her mother's request.

'I was getting bored,' she said. 'Same thing day after day.'

'You certainly won't get that with Amos,' Janine had remarked.

She was right. After only a few days Freya remarked, 'It's like dealing with a spoilt child. Don't worry. I can do what's necessary.'

Luckily, Amos liked his stepdaughter and under her care his health improved. It was she who now came bouncing out onto the balcony and said, 'Time for your nap.'

'Not for another ten minutes,' he growled.

She smiled. 'No, it's now. No argument.'

He grinned. 'You're a bully, you know that?'

'Of course I know that. I work at it. Get going.'

He shrugged, resigned and good-natured, and let her

escort him as far as his bedroom door. Janine would have gone in with him, but he waved her away.

'I can manage without supervision. Just keep your eyes open for Darius. I can't think what's keeping him.' He closed the door.

'What's going on?' Freya asked as the two women walked away.

'Goodness knows. He was supposed to arrive this morning but he called to say there'd been an unexpected delay.'

'And then all the other sons, Leonid, Marcel, Travis, Jackson, just a few days apart. Why is Amos suddenly doing this?'

'I can only guess,' Janine said sadly. 'He puts on this big act of being fully recovered, but he had a scare. He's seen that his life could end at any time, and he's…getting things sorted out, is how he puts it, starting with changes to his will.'

'Funny, he's so organised that you'd think he'd have fixed that ages ago.'

'He did, but I believe he's taking another look at all of his lads and deciding—I don't know—which one will manage best—'

'Which one is most like him,' Freya said shrewdly.

'You're very hard on him,' Janine protested.

'No more than he deserves. Of all the arrogant—'

'But he's very fond of you. You're the daughter he never had and he'd love you to be really part of the family.' She paused delicately.

'You mean he wants me to be his daughter-in-law?' Freya demanded, aghast. 'The cheeky crook.'

'Don't call him a crook,' Janine protested.

'Why not? No man builds up the kind of fortune he did by honest means. And he's taught his sons to be the same.

Anything for money, that's how they all think. So if one of them can talk me into marriage he'll cop the lot. Was Amos mad when he thought of that? Nothing on this earth would persuade me—there isn't one of them I'd ever dream of—ye gods and little fishes!'

'Don't tell him I told you,' Janine begged.

'Don't worry. Not a word.' Suddenly her temper faded, replaced by wicked mischief. 'But I might enjoy a good laugh. Yes, I think it deserves that.'

As she hurried away her mother heard the laughter echoing back, and sighed. She couldn't blame Freya one bit. She, of all people, knew what madness it was to marry into this family.

Darius arrived the next day, apologising with a fictional tale of business dealings. Not for the world would he have admitted that he'd been forced to leave Herringdean, return to the mainland and check into a hotel to put on a fresh suit. Normally, no power on earth could force him to change his plans and he resented it. Another thing for which Harriet Connor was to blame.

He found her mysteriously disturbing because she seemed to haunt him as two people. There was the girl who'd briefly charmed him with her instinctive empathy for his feelings about the isolated place. And there was the other one who'd interfered with his plans, destroyed his dignity with her stupid hound, and committed the unforgivable crime of seeing him at a disadvantage. He had dismissed her from his mind but she seemed unaware of that fact and popped up repeatedly in one guise or another.

A fanciful man might have defined her two aspects as the Good Fairy and the Bad Fairy. Darius, who wasn't fanciful, simply called her 'that wretched female'.

His father greeted him in typical fashion. 'So there you are at last. About time too.'

'An unexpected matter that required my attention.'

Amos grunted. 'As long as you sorted it out to your advantage.'

'Naturally,' Darius said, brushing aside the memory of lying on the sand. 'Then I got here as soon as I could. I'm glad to see you looking better, Father.'

'I *am* better. I keep saying so but my womenfolk won't believe me. I suppose Freya talked a lot when she collected you from the airport.'

'I asked her questions and, like a good nurse, she answered them.'

'Nurse be damned. She's here as my stepdaughter.'

'If you say so.'

'What do you think of her?'

'She seems a nice girl, what little I've seen of her.'

'She cheers the place up. And she's a good cook. Better than that so-called professional I employ. She's doing supper for us tonight. You'll enjoy it.'

He did enjoy it. Freya produced excellent food, and could crack jokes that lightened the atmosphere. She was pleasant to have around, and Darius found himself wondering why more women couldn't be like her instead of invading other people's private property with their sharp remarks and their dangerous dogs.

Awkward. She'd said it herself, and that was exactly right.

After supper, in his father's study, the two men confronted each other.

'I gather things aren't too good?' Amos grunted.

'Not for me or anyone else,' Darius retorted. 'There's a global crisis, hadn't you heard?'

'Yes, and some are weathering it better than others. That

contract you had the big fight over, I warned you how to word the get-out clause, and if you'd listened to me you could have told them where to stuff their legal action.'

'But they're decent people,' Darius protested. 'They knew very little about business—'

'All the better. You could have done as you liked and they wouldn't have found out until too late. You're soft, that's your trouble.'

Darius grimaced. In the financial world, his reputation was far from soft. Cold, unyielding, power-hungry, that was what people said of him. But he drew the line at taking advantage of helpless innocence, and he'd paid the price for it; a price his father would never have paid.

'But it's not too late,' Amos conceded in a milder tone. 'Now you're here there are ways I can help.'

'That's what I hoped,' Darius said quietly.

'You haven't always taken my advice, but perhaps you've got the sense to take it now. And the first problem is how you're going to deal with Morgan Rancing.'

'I must tell you—'

'I've heard disturbing rumours about some island he owns off the south coast of England. They say he'll try to use it to cover his debts, and I'm warning you to have no truck with that. Don't give it a thought. What you must do—'

'It's too late,' Darius growled. 'Herringdean is already mine.'

'What? You agreed to take it?'

'No, I wasn't given the chance,' Darius snapped. 'Rancing has vanished. Next thing, I received papers that transferred ownership of Herringdean to me. His cellphone is dead, his house is empty. Nobody knows where he is, or if they do they're not talking. I can either accept the island or go without anything.'

'But it'll be more trouble than it's worth,' Amos spluttered.

'I'm inclined to agree with you,' Darius murmured.

'So you know something about it?'

'A little. I need to go back and inspect it further.'

'And you're counting on it to pay your debts?'

'I don't know. But in the meantime I could do with an investor to make a one-time injection of cash and help me out.'

'Meaning me?'

'Well, as you're always telling me, you've survived the credit crunch better than anyone.'

'Yes, because I knew how to treat money.'

'Like a prisoner who's always trying to escape,' Darius recalled.

'Exactly. That's why I came to live here.'

He pushed open the door that led out onto the balcony overlooking the view over the bay that now glittered with lights against the darkness.

'I talked to a journalist once,' Amos recalled. 'She asked me all sorts of tom-fool questions. Why had I chosen to live in Monte Carlo? Was it just the tax relief or was there something else? I brought her out here and became lyrical about the view.'

'That I would have loved to hear,' Darius said.

Amos grinned. 'Yeah, you'd have been proud of me. The silly woman swallowed it hook, line and sinker. Then she wrote some trash about my being a man who appreciated peace and beauty. As though I gave a damn about that stuff.'

'Some people think it has value,' Darius murmured.

'Some people are fools,' Amos said firmly. 'I'd be sorry to think you were one of them. You've got yourself into a mess and you need me to get you out.'

'Two firms I did business with went bankrupt, owing me money,' Darius said grimly. 'I hardly created the mess myself.'

'But you made it worse by giving Mary everything she asked for in the divorce settlement.'

'That was before the crisis. I could afford it then.'

'But you didn't leave yourself any room for manoeuvre, no way to claw any of it back. You forgot every lesson I ever taught you. Now you want me to pour good money after bad.'

'So you won't help me?'

'I didn't say that, but we need to talk further. Not now. Later.'

Darius spoke through gritted teeth. 'Will my father invest in me, or will he not?'

'Don't rush me.'

'I have to. I need to make my decisions quickly.'

'All right, here's a way forward for you to consider. A rich wife, that's what you need, one who'll bring you a thumping great dowry.'

'What the hell are you talking about?'

'Freya. She's already my stepdaughter, and I want her properly in the family as my daughter-in-law.'

Darius stared. His ears were buzzing, and somewhere there was the memory of Freya, on the drive from the airport, saying, 'Your father's got some really mad ideas. Someone needs to tell him to forget them.'

She'd refused to elaborate, but now he understood.

'Why not?' Amos asked genially. 'You like the girl, you were laughing together at dinner—'

'Yes, I like her—far too much to do her such an injury, even if she'd agree, which she wouldn't, thank goodness. Do you really think you could make me crawl to do your bidding? If I have one thing left it's my independence, and I won't part with that.'

'Then you'll buy it at a high price. Don't blame me when you go bankrupt.'

Darius gave a cold smile. 'I'll remember.'

He turned and walked away, resisting the temptation to slam the door. Within an hour he'd left the house.

CHAPTER TWO

THE storm that swept over Herringdean had been violent, and nobody was surprised when the lifeboat was called out to an emergency. A small crowd had watched the boat plunge down the slipway into the sea, and a larger one gathered to see it return later that night.

Soon the rescued victims had been taken ashore into the waiting ambulance and the crew were free to exhale with relief and remove their life jackets.

Harriet took out her cellphone, dialled and spoke quickly. 'Is he all right? Good. I'll be home soon.'

When they had all finished making their report she slipped away and was followed by Walter and Simon, fellow crew members and friends.

'Hey, Harry,' Walter called. 'You sounded worried on the phone. Is someone ill?'

'No, I was just checking on Phantom. I left my neighbour looking after him. She promised to keep him safe.'

'Safe? Why suddenly? You never worried before.'

'I never had cause before. But now I worry. He's a very powerful man.'

'Who?'

From her pocket she took a newspaper cutting with a photograph and passed it to Walter.

'"Darius Falcon,"' he read. '"Giant of commerce, skilled

manipulator, the financial world is agog to know if he will avert disaster—'" He lowered the paper. 'How does a big shot come to know Phantom?'

'Because he's bought the island,' she said. 'Rancing had money troubles and he solved them by selling this place.'

Simon swore. 'And not a word to the people who live here, of course.'

'Of course. What do we matter to men like that, up there on their lofty perch? If you could have seen him as I did, arrogant and sure of himself—'

'You've met him?' Simon demanded.

'He came here a couple of days ago and I saw him on the beach. Phantom made a mess of his suit and he got mad, said he'd make me pay for a new one, and Phantom shouldn't be allowed out. So tonight, I asked my neighbour to watch over him while I was away, in case...well, just in case.'

'Hell!' Walter said. 'But is he really as bad as you say? If you two had a dust-up he probably just got a bit peeved—'

'You didn't see his face. He was more than a bit peeved. Now, I must get home.'

She hurried away, leaving the two men gazing after her, frowning with concern.

'Surely she's overreacting?' Simon mused. 'A bodyguard for a dog? A bit melodramatic, surely?'

'She's been that way for the last year,' Walter sighed. 'Ever since her husband died. Remember how good she and Brad were together? The perfect marriage. Now all she has left is his dog.'

'Hmm,' Simon grunted. 'Personally, I never liked Brad.'

'You say that because you fancied her rotten.'

'Sure, me and every other man on the island. Let's go for a drink.'

* * *

Harriet's car made quick time from the harbour to Ellarick, then to the little shop that she owned, and above which she lived. As she looked up the window opened and Phantom's head appeared, followed by that of a cheerful middle-aged woman. A moment later she was climbing the stairs to throw her arms about the dog.

'Mmm,' she cooed, and he responded with a throaty growl that sounded much the same.

'No problems?' she asked Mrs Bates, the neighbour who'd kept watch in her home.

'No sign of anyone.'

'Let me make you a cup of tea,' Harriet offered gratefully.

But Mrs Bates refused and departed. She was a kindly soul and she knew Harriet wanted to be alone with Phantom, although how she could bear the loneliness of the apartment Mrs Bates couldn't imagine.

But to Harriet it would never be lonely while Phantom was there. She hugged him fiercely before saying, 'Come on, let's take a walk. You need space to go mad in.'

They slipped out together into the darkness and walked down through the streets of the town, heading for the shore.

'But not "the ogre's" private beach,' she said. 'From now on, that's out of bounds.'

They found a place on the public sands where they could chase each other up and down in the moonlight.

'That's enough,' she gasped at last. 'Yes, I know you could go on till morning, but I'm out of puff.'

She threw herself down on the sand and stretched out on her back. Phantom immediately put a heavy paw on her chest, looking down into her face while she ruffled his fur.

'That's better,' she sighed. 'How could he not like you

when you were trying so hard to be friendly? Being hurled to the ground by you is a real privilege. You don't do it for everyone.' She gave a soft grunt of laughter. 'Just people with expensive clothes. If he really does send me the bill you'll be on plain rations for a long time. So will I, come to think of it.'

He woofed.

'The funny thing is, when I first saw him…he seemed decent, as if he really loved the sun and the fresh air; like someone who'd found himself in heaven. But when I discovered who he was he looked different. And then he was so rotten to you—'

Suddenly she sat up and threw her arms around the dog.

'You must be careful,' she said fiercely. 'You must, you *must*! If anything happened to you I couldn't bear it.'

Harriet buried her face against him. Phantom made a gentle sound, but he didn't try to move. This often happened, and he knew what he must do: keep still, stay warm and gentle, just be there for her. Instinct told him what she needed, and his heart told him how to give it.

'They think I'm crazy,' she whispered, 'getting paranoid over your safety. Well, perhaps I really am crazy, but you're all I've got—without you, there's no love or happiness in the world…only you…'

She kissed him and gave a shaky laugh.

'I expect you think I'm crazy too. Poor old boy. Come on, let's get home and you can have something special to eat.'

They left the beach, climbing the gently sloping road that led to the town. Suddenly she stopped. Far away, she could just make out the house where Rancing had lived before he fled, and where 'the ogre' would soon appear. It went by the grandiose name of Giant's Beacon, which might have been justified in its great days, but seemed rather over-the-top now that it was in a state of disrepair. At this distance it was tiny, but it stood out against the moonlit sky, and she could just make out that lights were coming on.

'He's here,' she breathed. 'Oh, heavens, let's get home, fast.'

They ran all the way, and as soon as they were safely inside Harriet locked the door.

Within hours of Darius's arrival the news had spread throughout the island. Kate, who'd kept house for Rancing, had a ready audience in the pub that evening.

'You should see the computers he's brought,' she said. 'Dozens of 'em. One for this and one for that, and something he calls "video links" so he can talk to people on the other side of the world, and there they are on the screen, large as life. It's like magic.'

The others grinned. Kate had never quite come to terms with the dot-com revolution, and most modern communications struck her as magic. She had little idea that behind its sweet, traditional image Herringdean was a more modern place than it looked.

Darius was also making the discovery, and was delighted with it. For a while he would be able to run his main business and his many subsidiary businesses, controlling everything from the centre of the web. It would be enough until he was ready to turn this place to his financial advantage.

Checking through the figures, he discovered that it was larger than he'd thought, about a hundred square miles with a population of a hundred and twenty thousand. Sheep and dairy farming flourished, so did fishing, and there were several industries, notably boat building and brewing.

Ellarick was not only a flourishing town, but a port with its own annual regatta.

One source of prosperity was tourism. Now summer was coming, the hotels were filling up as visitors began to flood the island, seeking tranquillity in the country lanes or excitement in the boats.

Ellarick also contained an elderly accountant called James Henly, who had dealt with Rancing's business. An early visit from him pleased Darius with the news that the rent paid to him by the other inhabitants was considerable, but also displeased him with the discovery that he was the victim of yet another piece of sharp practice.

'Mr Rancing persuaded several of his larger tenants, like the breweries, to pay him several months' rent in advance,' Henly explained in his dry voice. 'Apparently, he convinced them that there would be tax advantages. I need hardly say that I knew nothing about this. I was away and he took advantage of my absence to act on his own account. When I returned and found out, it was too late. He'd pocketed the money, and within a few days he'd vanished.'

'Meaning that it will be some time before I can collect rent from these establishments again,' Darius said in a mild manner that revealed nothing.

'I'm afraid so. Of course, what he's done is legally open to question since he made over everything to you, so technically it was your money he took. You could always try to get it back.'

His tone made it clear that he didn't attach much hope to that idea. Darius, who attached none at all, controlled his temper. It wasn't his way to display emotion to employees.

'How much are we talking about?' he said with a shrug.

He felt less like shrugging when he saw the figures.

Rancing had staged a spectacular theft and there was nothing he could do about it. But at all costs Henly mustn't be allowed to suspect his dismay.

'No problem,' Darius said as indifferently as he could manage. 'The tourism season is just starting. I shan't let a detail get me down.'

Henly's eyes widened at the idea of such a financial blow being a mere detail. He began to think the stories of Mr Falcon's impending ruin were untrue after all.

Darius, who'd intended him to think exactly that, asked casually, 'Did he leave owing you any money?'

'I'm afraid he did—'

'All right, just send me a detailed bill. That's all for now.'

For several days he remained in the house, rising early to link up with business contacts on one side of the world, eating whatever Kate brought him and barely taking his eyes from the computer screen. As the hours wore on, he turned to the other side of the world where he had business contacts whose day was just beginning. Day and night ceased to exist; all he knew was what he needed to do to survive.

On a whim, he searched the local phone directory until he found Harriet Connor, living in Bayton Street in Ellarick. A map showed him that it was in the centre of the town.

Then he put away the papers quickly. What did he care where she lived?

Thinking back to his work, at last he felt he'd put things on a firmer footing and could dare to hope. Perhaps it was time to venture outside. He'd hired a car but so far not used it. Now he drove into Ellarick, parked in a side street and got out to walk.

No doubt it was pure chance that made him walk down Bayton Street. He reckoned that must have been the reason because he'd forgotten her address. Now he found himself in a place of expensive shops and hotels that looked even more expensive. The tourist trade must be good. No doubt she did well out of the hotels.

There was her shop, on the corner, and through the open door he could just see her with a female customer. There was a child there too, and Harriet was talking to the little boy, giving him all her attention, as though nobody else mattered. He was clutching a large model boat, and Darius saw him turn to the woman and say, 'Please, Mum. *Please.*'

He could just make out her reply, 'No, darling, it's too expensive.'

For a moment the child looked rebellious, but then he sniffed and handed the boat to Harriet. She took it thoughtfully, then suddenly said, 'I could always make a discount.'

The mother gasped, and gasped again when she saw the piece of paper on which Harriet had written the price. 'Are you sure?'

'Quite sure. It ought to go to someone who'll really appreciate it.'

Darius moved quickly back into a doorway as the woman paid up and hurried away with the child. The last thing he wanted was for Harriet to realise that he'd witnessed this scene. Instinct told him that she wouldn't be pleased at knowing he'd seen her kindly side any more than he would be at knowing she'd seen his. Not that he admitted to having a kindly side.

He waited until she put up the shutters before hurrying back to the car.

The following night he was out walking again, much later this time. Darkness had fallen as he headed for the harbour. At last he came to a public house and went inside, only to find the place too crowded for his mood.

'It's nice outside,' the barman suggested. 'Plenty of space there.'

He led Darius to the garden, where a few tables were laid out. From one of them came laughter.

'We're near the lifeboat station,' the barman explained, 'so the crew members tend to come in here to relax after a call out. That's them, just there.'

He pointed to where two women and four men were sitting around a table, laughing and talking. They were well lit, but then the lights faded into darkness, tempting Darius to slip in among the trees, hoping to remain unseen. From here he could catch a distant glimpse of the sea, that mysteriously always had the power to make him feel better.

A cheer rose from the table, making him back away, but not before he'd seen who was sitting there, surrounded by laughing admirers.

It was her. The Bad Fairy. Or was she now the Good Fairy? He wished she'd let him make up his mind.

The man beside her put a friendly hand on her shoulder, roaring, 'Harry, you're a fraud.'

'Of course I'm a fraud, Walter,' she teased back. 'That's the only fun thing to be.'

Harriet, he remembered. Harry.

Was there no escape from the pesky woman? Why here and now, spoiling his quiet contemplation? And why was she wearing a polo shirt that proclaimed her a member of the lifeboat crew?

Phantom was at her feet, and Darius had a chance to study him. Before, he'd sensed only a very large dog of no particular breed. Now he could see that Phantom's ancestry included a German Shepherd, a St Bernard, and possibly a bloodhound. He was a handsome animal with a benign air that at any other time Darius would have appreciated. Now he only remembered the heavy creature pinning him to the ground and making a fool of him.

The crowd around the table were still chattering cheerfully.

'So what are we going to do about this guy who thinks he owns the place?' Walter asked.

'Actually, he really does own the place,' Harriet sighed. 'And there's nothing we can do. We're stuck with him, I'm sorry to say.'

A groan went up, and someone added, 'Apparently, he's spending money like there's no tomorrow, yet according to the newspapers he's a poor man now. Go figure.'

'Hah!' Harriet said cynically. 'What we call poor and what Darius Falcon calls poor would be a million miles apart.'

Now Darius was even more glad of the trees hiding him, so that they couldn't see his reaction to the contemptuous way she spoke his name.

'It's a big act,' she went on. 'He has to splash it around to prove he can afford to, but actually he's a fraud.'

'Gee, you really took against him!' said the other woman sitting at the same table. 'Just because he got mad at Phantom for ruining his suit. I adore Phantom, but let's face it, he's got form for that kind of thing.'

Amid the general laughter, Harriet made a face.

'It wasn't just that,' she said. 'It's also the way I first saw him, with his head thrown back, drinking in the sun.'

'Perhaps he just likes nature,' Walter suggested.

'That's what I thought. I even liked him for it, but then I didn't know who he was. Now I see. He was standing there like a king come into his birthright. He owns the land and he owns us, that's how he sees it.'

'He told you that?'

'He didn't need to. It was all there in his attitude.' She assumed a declamatory pose. 'I'm the boss here and you'd better watch out.'

'Now that I'd like to see,' said Walter. 'The last man who tried to boss you about was me, and you made me regret it.'

More cheers and laughter. Someone cracked a joke about Darius, someone else cracked another, while their victim stood in the shadows, fuming. This was another new experience and one Darius could have done without. Awe, respect, even fear, these he was used to. But derision? That was an insult.

Walter leaned towards her confidentially. 'Hey, Harry, make a note never to rescue him. If you find him in the water, do the world a favour and look the other way.'

Roars of laughter. She raised her glass, chuckling, 'I'll remember.'

That was it. Time for her to be taught a lesson.

Emerging from the trees, he approached the table and stood, watching her sardonically, until the others noticed him and became curious. At last Harriet's attention was caught and she turned. He heard her draw a sharp breath, and registered her look of dismay with grim satisfaction.

'You'd better remind yourself of my face,' he said, 'so that you'll know who to abandon.'

She couldn't speak. Only her expression betrayed her horror and embarrassment.

He should then have turned on his heel and departed without giving her a chance to reply. But Phantom had to spoil it. Recognising his new friend, he rose from where he was nestled beneath Harriet's seat and reared up, barking with delight.

'Phantom, no!' she cried.

'Leave him,' Darius told her, rubbing Phantom's head.

'You daft mutt! Is this how you get your fun? Luckily, I'm in casuals tonight. Now, get down, there's a good fellow.'

After Harriet's dire warnings, his relaxed tone took everyone by surprise and he noticed that puzzled frowns were directed at her. Fine. If she wanted battle, she could have it. He nodded to them all and departed.

When he reached the road he heard footsteps hurrying behind him and turned, half fearing another canine embrace. But it was her.

'That thing about leaving you in the sea—it was just a silly joke. Of course we'd never leave *anyone* to drown.'

'Not anyone,' he echoed. 'Meaning not even a monster like me.'

'Look—'

'Don't give it another thought. The chance of my ever needing to rely on you is non-existent—as you'll discover.'

'Oh, really!' she said, cross again. 'Let's hope you're right. You never know what life has in store next, do you? Let's make sure.'

Grabbing him, she yanked him under a street lamp and studied his face, frowning.

'You look different from last time,' she said. 'It must be the darkness. OK, I've got you fixed. Hey, what are you doing?'

'The same to you as you did to me,' he said, holding her with one hand while the other lifted her chin to give him the best view of her face.

Harriet resisted the temptation to fight him off, suspecting that he would enjoy that too much. Plus she guessed he wouldn't be easy to fight. There was an unyielding strength in his grasp that could reduce her to nothing. So she stayed completely still, outwardly calm but inwardly smouldering.

If only he would stop smiling like that, as though something about her both amused and pleased him. There was a gleam in his eyes that almost made her want to respond. Almost. If she was that foolish. She drew a long breath, trying not to tremble.

At last he nodded, saying in a thoughtful voice, 'Hmm. Yes, I think I'll remember you—if I try really hard.'

'*Cheek!*' she exploded.

He released her. 'All right, you can go now.'

Darius walked away without looking back. He didn't need to. He knew she was looking daggers at him.

At home in Giant's Beacon, he sat in darkness at the window of his room with a drink, trying to understand what had so disturbed him that night. It wasn't the hostility, something he was used to. Nor was it really the laughter, which had annoyed him, but only briefly. It was something about Harriet—something…

He exhaled a long breath as the answer came to him. She'd spoken of seeing him on the beach, 'standing there like a king come into his birthright.'

That hadn't been her first reaction. She'd even said she'd liked him, but only briefly, until she'd discovered who he was. Then she'd seen only arrogance and harshness, a conqueror taking possession.

But wasn't that partly his own choice? For years he'd assumed various masks—cool, unperturbed, cunning, superior or charming when the occasion warranted it. Some had been passed on to him by a father whose skill in manipulation was second to none. Others he'd created for himself.

Only one person had seen a different side of him—loving, passionate. For twelve years he'd enjoyed what he'd thought of as a happy marriage, until his wife had left him for another man. Since then he'd tried to keep the vulnerable face well hidden, but evidently he should try harder.

He snatched up the phone and dialled his ex-wife's number in London.

'Mary?'

'Do you have to ring me at this hour? I was just going to bed.'

'I suppose *he's* with you?'

'That's no longer any concern of yours, since we're divorced.'

'Are Mark and Frankie there?'

'Yes, but they're asleep and I'm not waking them. Why don't you call during the day, *if you can make time?* I never liked having to wait until you'd finished everything else, and they don't like it either.'

'Tell them I'll call tomorrow.'

'Not during the day. It's a family outing.'

'When you say "family" I take it you mean—'

'Ken, too. You shouldn't be surprised. We'll be married soon, and he'll be their father.'

'The hell he will! I'll call tomorrow evening. Tell them to expect me.' He slammed down the phone.

Darius had a fight on his hands there, he knew it. Mary had been a good wife and mother, but she'd never really understood the heavy demands of his work. And now, if he wasn't careful, she would cut his children off from him.

How his enemies would rejoice at his troubles. Enemies. In the good times they had been called opponents, rivals, competitors. But the bad times had changed all that, bringing out much bile and bitterness that had previously been hidden for tactical reasons.

As so often, Harriet was hovering on the edge of his mind, an enemy who was at least open about her hostility. Tonight he'd had the satisfaction of confronting her head-on, a rare pleasure in his world. He could see her now, cheeky and challenging, but not beautiful, except for her eyes, and with skin that was as soft as rose petals; something that he'd discovered when he'd held her face prisoner between his fingers.

This was how he'd always fought the battles, gaining information denied to others. But now it was different. Instead of triumph, he felt only confusion.

After watching the darkness for a long time he went to bed.

CHAPTER THREE

HARRIET prided herself on her common sense. She needed to. There had been times in her recent past when it had been all that saved her from despair. Even now, the dark depths sometimes beckoned and she clung fiercely to her 'boring side' as she called it, because nothing else helped. And even that didn't make the sadness go away. It simply made it possible to cling on until her courage returned.

She knew that people had always envied her. Married at eighteen to an astonishingly handsome young man, living in apparently perfect harmony until his death eight years later. As far as the world knew, the only thing that blighted their happiness was the need for him to be away so often. His work in the tourist industry had necessitated many absences from home, but when he returned their reunions were legendary.

'A perfect couple,' people said. But they didn't know.

Brad had been a philanderer who had spent his trips away sleeping around, and expected her not to mind. It only happened while he was out of sight, so what was she complaining about? It was the unkindness of his attitude that hurt her as much as his infidelity.

She'd clung on, deluding herself with the hope that in time he would change, presenting a bright face to the world so that her island neighbours never suspected. Finally Brad had left her, dying in a car crash in America before the divorce could come through, and the last of her hope was destroyed.

To the outside world the myth of her perfect marriage persisted. Nobody knew the truth, and nobody ever would, she was determined on that.

All she had left was Phantom, who had been Brad's dog and who'd comforted her night after night when he was away. Phantom alone knew the truth; that behind the cheerful, sturdy exterior was a woman who had lost faith in men and life. His warmth brought joy to what would otherwise have been a desert.

It was the thought of her beloved dog that made her set out one morning in the direction of Giant's Beacon. There was still a chance to improve relations with Darius Falcon, and for Phantom's sake she must take it.

'I suppose I'm getting paranoid about this,' she told herself. 'I don't think he'd really do anything against Phantom, but he's the most powerful man on the island and I can't take chances.'

She recalled that at their last meeting he'd actually spoken to him in a kindly tone, calling him 'You daft mutt' and 'a good fellow', thus proving he wasn't really a monster. He probably had a nicer side if she could only find it. She would apologise, engage him in a friendly chat and all would be well.

The road to Giant's Beacon led around the side of the house, and over the garden hedge she could see that the French windows were open. From inside came the sound of a man's voice.

'All right. Call me again when you know. Goodbye.'

Excellent, she would slip inside quickly while he was free. But as she approached the open door she heard him again,'There you are. I know you've been avoiding my calls—did you really think I'd let you go that easily?—I know what you've been doing and I'm telling you it's got to stop.'

Harriet stood deadly still, stunned by his cold, bullying tone. She must leave at once. Slowly, she flattened herself back against the wall and began to edge away.

'It's too late for that,' Darius continued. 'I've set things in motion and it's too late to change it, even if I wanted to. The deal's done, and you can tell your friend with the suspicious credentials that if he crosses me again he'll be sorry—what? Yes, that's exactly what I mean. There'll be no mercy.'

No mercy, she thought, moving slowly along the wall. That just about said it all. And she'd kidded herself that he had a nicer side.

No mercy.

Quietly, she vanished.

'There'll be no mercy.'

Darius repeated the line once more. He knew that these days he said it too often, too obsessively. So many foes had shown him no mercy that now it was the mantra he clung to in self-defence.

At last he slammed down the phone and threw himself back in his chair, hoping he'd said enough to have the desired impact. Possibly. Or then again, maybe not. Once he wouldn't have doubted it, but since his fortunes had begun to collapse he had a permanent fear that the person on the other end immediately turned to a companion and jeered, 'He fell for it.'

As he himself had often done in what now felt like another life.

That was one of the hardest things to cope with— the suspicion of being laughed at behind his back; the knowledge that people who'd once scuttled to please him now shrugged.

The other thing, even harder, was the end of his family life, the distance that seemed to stretch between himself and his children. It was easy to say that he'd given too much of himself to business and not enough to being a father, but at the time he'd felt he was working for them.

Mary, his wife, had been scathing at the idea.

'That's just your excuse for putting them second. You say making money is all for them, but they don't want a great fortune, they want *you* there, taking an interest.'

He'd sacrificed so much for financial success, and now that too was fading. Lying awake at night, he often tried to look ahead to decide which path to take, but in truth there was no choice. Only one path stretched forward, leading either to greater failure or success at too great a cost. They seemed much the same.

He rubbed his eyes, trying to shake off the mood, and turned on the radio to hear the local news. One item made him suddenly alert.

'Much concern is being expressed at the suggestion of problems with the Herringdean Wind Farm. Work has only recently started, yet—'

'Kate,' he said, coming downstairs, 'what do you know about a wind farm?'

'Not much,' she said, speaking as she would have done about an alien planet. 'It's been on and off for ages and we thought it was all forgotten but they finally started work. It'll be some way out in the channel where we don't have to look at the horrid great thing.'

'Show me,' he said, pulling out a map of the island.

The site was located about eight miles out at sea, within

England's territorial waters. As these were owned by the Crown, he would gain nothing. He could even lose, since the island might be less appealing to potential buyers.

'They've actually started putting up the turbines?' he said.

'A few, I believe, but it'll be some time before it's finished.'

He groaned. If he'd bought this place in the normal way, there would have been inspections, he would have discovered the disadvantages and negotiated a lower price. Instead, it had been dumped on him, and he was beginning to realise that he'd walked into a trap.

Fool! *Fool!*

At all costs that must remain his secret. Kate was too naïve for him to worry about, and nobody else would be allowed near.

'Shall I start supper?' Kate asked.

'No, thank you. There's something I've got to see.'

Darius had just enough time to get out there before the light faded. When he'd inspected the turbines he could decide if they were a problem.

For this he would need the motorboat that was also now his property, and that was lodged in a boating shed at the end of a small creek that ran in from the shore. He found it without trouble, opened the door of the shed and started up the engine.

He was expecting problems. The engine might not work, or would at least be complicated to operate. But it sprang to life at once, everything was easy to operate, and since the fuel gauge registered 'full' he reckoned that luck was on his side, just for once.

Briefly he glanced around for a life jacket but, not seeing one, shrugged and forgot about it. A breeze was getting up as he emerged from the creek and set out across the channel. Glancing back, he could see the beach where he'd had his first ill-fated meeting with Harriet. Then he turned determinedly away and headed for the horizon.

At last he saw it—a dozen turbines rearing out of the water, seventy metres high, and, nearby, the cargo ships bearing the loads that would become more turbines. He got as close as he could, trying to think only of the benefit to the island of this source of electricity. But the new self, who'd come to life on the beach, whispered that they spoiled the beauty of the sea.

Functional and efficient, that was what mattered. Concentrate on that.

Now the light was fading fast and the wind was mounting, making the water rough, and it was time to go. He turned the boat, realising that he'd been unwise to come out here. He wasn't an experienced sailor, but the need to know had been compelling. Now he had just enough time to get to shore before matters became unpleasant.

Almost at once he discovered his mistake. The waves mounted fast, tossing his little boat from side to side. Rain began to fall more heavily every moment, lashing the angry water, lashing himself, soaking through his clothes, which weren't waterproof. The sooner he drove on the better.

But without warning the engine died. Nothing he could do would start it again. Frantically, he peered at the fuel gauge and saw, with horror, that it still showed 'Full'.

But that was impossible after the distance he'd already travelled. The reading was wrong, and must have been wrong from the start. He'd set out without enough fuel, and now he was trapped out here in the storm.

He groaned. It went against the grain to admit that he needed help, but there was no alternative. He would have to call Kate and ask her to notify the rescue service. Then it would be all over the island. He could almost hear the laughter. Especially *hers*. But it couldn't be helped.

Taking out his cellphone, he began to dial, trying to steady himself with his feet as he needed both hands for the phone. That was when the biggest wave came, rearing up at the side of the boat, forcing him to cling on with both hands. With despair, he saw the phone go flying into the water. He made a dive for it but another swell hoisted the boat high, twisting it so that he went overboard into the sea.

Floundering madly, he tried to reach the boat, but the waves had already carried it away. Farther and farther away it went, beyond his strength to pursue, until it was out of sight.

Now his own body seemed to be turning against him. The shock of being plunged into cold water had caused his heart to race dangerously, making him gasp and inhale water. His limbs froze, and he could barely move them. He wondered whether he would die of cold before he drowned.

Time passed, tormenting him, then vanishing into eternity until time itself no longer existed. Perhaps it had never existed. There was only darkness on earth and the moon and stars high above.

His wretchedness was increased by the thought of his children, waiting in vain for his call tonight. They would think he'd forgotten them, and only the news of his death would tell them otherwise. Then it would no longer matter.

Darius wanted to cry aloud to them, saying he loved them and they must believe that, for he would never be able to tell them again. But the distance stretched into infinity, and then another infinity that he feared because so much was left undone in his life—so many wrongs not righted,

so many chances not taken, so many words not spoken...
and now...never...never...

Why was he even bothering to tread water? Why not
just let go and accept the inevitable?

But giving in had never been his way. He must fight to
the end, no matter how much harder it was.

In his dizzy state he seemed to lose consciousness. Or
was he going mad? That might make it easier. But doing
things the easy way wasn't his style either.

Yet the madness was already creeping over him, giving
him the illusion of lights in the distance. It was impossible
but he saw them, streaming out over the water, turning this
way and that as though searching. Then the beam fell on
him, blinding him, and a cry split the darkness.

'There he is!'

The universe seemed to whirl. Vaguely, he sensed the
boat approaching, ploughing through the waves. Another
few seconds—

But it seemed that a malign fate was intent on destroying
him even now. A wave, bigger than the others, reared up,
sweeping him with it, up—then down back into the abyss—
up—down—then away from the boat to a place where he
would never be found. A yell of fear and rage broke from
him at being defeated at the last moment.

Then he felt a hand clasp his, the fingers tightening with
fierce determination, drawing him closer. The waves fought
back but the hand refused to yield to them. Suddenly he
realised that two men were in the water with him, and were
loading him onto a stretcher. Gradually the stretcher began
to rise, taking him clear of the sea, lifting him to safety.

From somewhere a man's voice said, 'OK, I've got him.
You can let go, Harry.'

And a woman replied, "No way. This one's mine.'

Harry! That voice—

Shocked, he opened his eyes and saw Harriet's face.

'You,' he whispered hoarsely.

Harriet was there, leaning close to ask, 'Was there anyone else with you—anyone we still need to look for?'

'No,' he gasped. 'I was alone.'

'Good. Then we can go back. There'll be an ambulance to take you to hospital.'

'No, I must go home—my children—I've got to call them. Wait—' he grasped her '—my cellphone went into the water. Let me use yours.'

'I don't have it here.'

'Then I must call them from home.'

'But the hospital will have—'

'Not the hospital,' he said stubbornly.

'Gee, you're an infuriating man!' she exclaimed.

'Yes, well, you should have left me in the water, shouldn't you?' he choked. 'You had the right idea the first time.'

A coughing fit overtook him. Between them, Harriet and Walter got him under cover, and she stayed with him for the rest of the journey. He slumped in the seat, his eyes closed, on the verge of collapse. Watching him, Harriet was glad she hadn't needed to answer his last remark. She wouldn't have known how.

At the lifeboat station she helped him ashore, and there was another argument.

'No hospital,' he insisted. 'I'm going home.'

'Then I'll take you,' she said. 'Walter—'

'Don't worry, I'll do the report. You keep him safe.'

Darius was about to say that he would drive himself when he remembered that his car was a mile away. Besides, there was no arguing with this bossy woman.

Somehow, he stumbled into her car and sat with his eyes closed for the journey.

'How did you manage to find me?' he murmured. 'I thought I was a goner.'

'Kate raised the alarm. She said you left suddenly after you talked about the wind farm. Later, she went out and bumped into an old man she knows who works on the shore. He said he'd seen you leaving in your motorboat. When you didn't return she tried to call you on your cellphone, but it was dead so she alerted the lifeboat station.'

Kate was waiting at the door when they arrived. Darius managed to stand up long enough to hug her.

'Thank you,' he said hoarsely. 'I owe you my life.'

'As long as you're safe,' Kate insisted. 'Just come in and get warm.'

In the hall, he made straight for the phone.

'Get changed,' Harriet said urgently. 'You're soaking.'

'No, I've got to call them first. They'll be waiting.' He'd been dialling as he spoke and now he said, 'Mary? Yes, I know it's late. I'm sorry, I got held up.'

From where she was standing, Harriet could hear a woman's sharp voice on the other end, faint but clear.

'You always get held up. The children went to bed crying because you didn't keep your word, and that's it. Enough is enough.'

'Mary, listen—'

'I'm not going to let you hurt them by putting them last again—'

'It's not like that—*don't hang up*—'

Harriet couldn't stand it any more. She snatched the phone from his hand and spoke loudly. 'Mrs Falcon, please listen to me.'

'Oh, you're the girlfriend, I suppose?'

'No, I'm not Mr Falcon's girlfriend. I'm a member of the lifeboat crew that's just taken him from the sea, barely in time to save his life.'

'Oh, please, do you expect me to believe that?'

Harriet exploded with rage. 'Yes, I do expect you to believe it because it's true. If we'd got there just a few minutes later it would have been too late. You're lucky he's here and not at the bottom of the ocean.' She handed the phone to Darius, who was staring as though he'd just seen an apparition. 'Tell her,' she commanded.

Dazed, he took the receiver and spoke into it. 'Mary? Are you still there?—yes, it's true what she said.'

A sense of propriety made Harriet back away in the direction of the kitchen but an overwhelming curiosity made her leave the door open just enough to eavesdrop.

'Please fetch them,' she heard him say. 'Oh, they've come downstairs? Let me talk to them. Frankie—is that you? I'm sorry about the delay—I fell in the water but they pulled me out—I'm fine now. Put Mark on, let me try and talk to both of you at once.'

His tone had changed, becoming warm and caressing in a way Harriet wouldn't have believed possible. Now she backed into the kitchen and shut the door, gratefully accepting a cup of tea from Kate.

'He'll go down with pneumonia if he doesn't get changed soon,' Kate observed worriedly.

'Then we'll have to be very firm with him,' Harriet said.

'Like you were just now.' Kate's tone was admiring. 'He didn't know what had hit him.'

'I suppose he'll be cross with me, but it can't be helped.'

'As long as we keep him safe,' Kate agreed.

Harriet look at her curiously. 'You sound as though you really care. But he can't be very easy to work for.'

'I'll take him rather than the last fellow any day. Rancing

just vanished, leaving me here for weeks. He never got in touch, never paid me—'

'Didn't pay you?' Harriet echoed, aghast. 'The lousy so-and-so. How did you live?'

'I had a little saved, but I had to spend it all. I couldn't contact him. Nothing. Then Mr Falcon walked in and said the place was his. I was still living here because I've got nowhere else to go. I thought he'd throw me out and bring in an army of posh servants, but he said he wanted me to stay and he paid me for all the weeks after Rancing left.'

'He—paid you? But—'

'I know. He didn't have to. He didn't owe me and I couldn't believe it when he handed me the cash.'

Harriet stared, feeling as though the world had suddenly turned upside down. This couldn't be true. Darius was a villain. That had been a settled fact in her mind. Until tonight—

'Why didn't you tell anyone?' she asked.

'Because he said not to. He'd be good and mad if he knew I'd told you now, so you'll keep quiet, won't you?'

'Of course. I'm not even quite convinced.'

'No, he said you wouldn't be.'

'He said what?'

'Not at the time, but last night when I was making his supper, I mentioned it, asked if I could tell people, and he said that you especially must never know because you enjoyed seeing him as the devil and he didn't want to spoil your fun.'

'Oh, *did* he?'

There were no words for the unfamiliar sensation that shook her. Darius had looked into her mind and read it with a precision that was alarming. Or exciting. She wasn't sure. One thing was certain. Everything she'd thought she knew about him was now in question. And the truth about his real nature was an even bigger question. The world had gone mad, taking her with it.

And what a journey that might be!

She recovered enough to say, 'But if people knew he could be as generous as this they'd see him differently.'

'Perhaps he doesn't want them to,' Kate said wisely.

That silenced Harriet. This was too much to take in all in one go. She needed space and solitude.

It was time to see how he was managing. Opening the door, they looked out into the hall and saw Darius sitting so still that they thought the call was ended, but then he said, 'All right,' in a hard voice.

After a pause he added, 'You'd better go back to bed now—yes, all right. Goodbye.'

He set the phone down and leaned back against the wood, eyes closed, face exhausted. Something told Harriet the call hadn't gone well.

'Time for bed,' Kate told him. 'Shall we help you up the stairs?'

'Thank you, but there's no need,' he growled.

He hauled himself slowly to his feet and began the weary trek, stair by stair, but waving the two women away if they seemed to get too close. They contented themselves with keeping a respectful distance, following him up and into his room, where he sat heavily on the bed.

'It's all right,' he said. 'I can manage.'

'No, you can't,' Harriet firmly. 'If we leave now you'll just stretch out and go to sleep in your freezing wet clothes. Next stop, pneumonia.'

'Now, look—'

'No, you look. I didn't give up my evening to come out to sea and fetch you to have you throw your life away through carelessness. You're going to take off those wet clothes and put on dry ones.'

Darius looked warily from one to the other, and seemed to decide against argument. His eyes closed and Harriet thought for a moment he would lose consciousness. But when he opened them again an incredible change seemed to come over him.

Astonished, Harriet saw a faint grin that might almost have been good-natured, or at least resigned. Then he shrugged.

'I'm in your hands, ladies.'

He unbuttoned his own shirt and shrugged it off, then unzipped his trousers and stood while they removed them. Kate fetched towels and a bathrobe that Harriet helped him put on. He tried to draw the edges together before removing his underpants, but his grip was weak and they fell open at the crucial moment.

Harriet quickly averted her eyes, but not before she'd seen his nakedness. Just a brief glimpse, but it told her what she didn't want to know, that his personal magnificence measured up to his reputation in business.

Hastily, she began opening drawers, asking, 'Where are your pyjamas?'

'I don't have any. Sleeping in the nude is more comfortable.' He raised an eyebrow at her. 'Don't you find that?'

'I really wouldn't know,' she said primly. It was incredible to her that he'd chosen this moment to tease her. He was half dead, for pity's sake! Did nothing crush him?

'I'm making you a hot tea,' she declared, 'and when I come back I expect to find you in bed.'

'Yes, ma'am,' he said meekly.

Now Harriet was sure she could see a gleam of humour far back in his eyes, but she couldn't be sure.

'I'll leave you in Kate's capable hands.' Some defensive instinct made her add, 'Don't stand any nonsense from him, Kate.'

'Don't you worry,' Kate said significantly.

'Harriet!' She turned at the door in response to Darius's voice. 'Thank you,' he said quietly.

'Don't mention it.'

She departed hurriedly. Downstairs, she made the tea but only took it halfway up the stairs before calling Kate and handing it to her. Suddenly it was important to escape him, above all to escape his knowing look that said he would tease her if he wanted to, and what was she going to do about it?

There was nothing to be done, except get back home—a place of safety, where she knew what was what.

When she got there safety greeted her in the form of Phantom. As they snuggled down under the covers she discussed the matter with him, as she discussed everything.

'What a night! Him of all people. And it seems he's not like... Well, I don't know what he's like any more. He was nice to Kate, I'll admit that. Maybe we were wrong about him. No, not we. Just me. You always liked him, didn't you?

'If you could have seen him getting undressed tonight. It was an honest accident—at least, I think it was. But what I saw was impressive and maybe he meant me to see and maybe he didn't.

'He ticks the boxes—great thighs, narrow hips and the rest—well, never mind. But Brad also ticked the boxes, and he *knew* he ticked them. A man like that wasn't going to confine himself to me, was he? And he didn't. So if His Majesty Falcon is expecting me to be impressed he can just think again.

'You agree with me, don't you? Well, you do if you want that new stuff I bought for your breakfast tomorrow. Yes—yes—that's a lovely lick. Can I have another? Thank you. Now, let's go to sleep. And move over. Give me some room.'

CHAPTER FOUR

HARRIET spent the next morning at her shop, which was doing well. She'd recently taken on a new assistant who was good at the job, something she was glad of when Kate rang, sounding frantic. 'Darius is driving me crazy wanting to do all sorts of daft things.'

'Hah! Surprise me.'

'He's got a nasty cold, but he insists on getting up. He says he's got to go out and buy another cellphone. He's ordered a fancy one online but it'll take a few days to arrive so he's determined to get something basic to fill in. And then he wants to come and see you.'

'All right, I'm on my way. Don't let him out. Tie him to the bed if you have to.'

Distantly, she heard Kate say, 'She says I'm to tie you to the bed,' followed by a sound that might have been a snort of laughter, followed by coughing.

'You hear that?' Kate demanded into the phone. 'If you—'

Her voice vanished, replaced by a loud burr. Harriet hung up, very thoughtful.

Before leaving, she took out an object that until then she'd kept hidden away and looked at it for a long time. At last she sighed and replaced it. But then, heading for the door, she stopped, returned and retrieved it from its hiding place. Again, she gazed at it for several moments, a yearning expression haunting her eyes. Her hand tightened on it and for a moment she seemed resolute. But then she returned it firmly to its hiding place, ran out of the room and downstairs, where she got into her car and began the journey to Giant's Beacon.

Halfway there she stopped, turned the car and swiftly headed back to streak up the stairs, snatch the precious object, ram it into her pocket and flee.

She'd done it now, the thing she'd vowed never to do, and that was that. She told herself it was time to be sensible, but she made the journey with her face set as though resisting pain

Kate was waiting for her on the doorstep, calling, 'Thank goodness you're here!'

'Kate, is that her?' cried a hoarse voice from the back of the house.

'I'm coming,' she called, hurrying into the room he'd turned into an office.

At first she was bewildered by the array of machinery, all of it obviously state-of-the-art. Kate had spoken of wonderful things, but still the variety and magnificence came as a surprise. And one man could control all this?

Darius, in his dressing gown, was sitting at a large screen, his fingers hovering over a keyboard.

'Don't come near me,' he croaked. 'I'm full of germs.'

'You shouldn't be up at all,' she scolded him, sitting down at a distance. 'And Kate says you want to go out. That's madness. It's far too cold.'

'I thought summer was supposed to be coming. Is it always like this in May?'

'The weather can be a bit temperamental. It's been colder than usual the last few days. It'll warm up soon, and then we'll be flooded with tourists. In the meantime, take care.'

'I just need a new cellphone to replace the one I lost last night. I have a thousand calls to make, and the house phone keeps going dead.'

'Yes, the line's faulty and they don't seem able to repair it. You were lucky it held out last night when you were calling your children. All right, you need one to tide you over. Try this.'

Reaching into her pocket, she handed over the object that had given her such anguish earlier.

'You're lending me yours?' he asked.

'No, it's not mine, it…belonged to my husband.'

He took it from her left hand, realising for the first time that she wore a wedding ring.

'Husband?' he echoed.

'He died a year ago. He hadn't used this for some time because he'd replaced it with a better one. But it might get you through the next few days.'

He seemed uncertain what to say.

'That's very kind of you,' he murmured at last. 'But—are you sure?'

'Quite sure. You'll find it blank. I've wiped off every trace of him.'

Something in her voice made him glance at her quickly, but she was looking out of the window.

'I appreciate this,' he said. 'Now I can call my children again. I'll be in touch as soon as I'm a bit more normal. I still have to thank you properly for saving me. Perhaps we could have dinner.'

'You don't need to thank me. I was just doing what I do and I wasn't alone. What about all the others on the lifeboat?'

'I'll show my gratitude by making a donation. But I

think you can tell me a lot about Herringdean that I need to know, so I'd appreciate it if you'd agree to dinner.'

'All right, I'll look forward to it.'

'By the way,' he added as she reached the door, 'how's my ghostly friend?'

'Who?'

'His name is Phantom, isn't it?'

She gave an uncertain laugh. 'You call him your friend?'

'You assured me he was only being friendly. Tell him I look forward to our next meeting. What kind of bones does he like?'

'Any kind.'

'I'll remember.'

As she left the house Harriet was saying to herself, 'I don't believe it. I imagined that conversation. I must have done.'

That evening she poured out her thoughts again to the one friend she knew she could always trust.

'I don't know what to think any more. He's different— well, all right, he nearly died and that changes people— but they change back. In a few days he'll be talking about showing no mercy again. Hey, don't do that! Phantom, *put that down!*—oh, all right, just this once.'

Three days later she looked up from serving in the shop to find Darius standing there.

'It's a nice day so I managed to escape,' he said with a smile. 'I wanted to bring you this.' He held out the phone. 'I've got my new one now, but this was invaluable. Thank you. There seems no end to what I owe you.'

'Did you manage to call your sons?'

'My son and daughter, yes.'

'Oh, I thought—Mark and Frank.'

'Frankie. Her name's Francesca, but we call her Frankie. It's a bit like calling you Harry.'

She laughed. 'Yes, I suppose it is.'

'And there's also this,' he said, reaching into a bag and drawing out a huge bone. 'This is for Phantom, by the way, not you.'

Her lips twitched. 'I'm glad you explained that.'

'About our dinner. Kate's set her heart on cooking it for us.'

'Good idea. She's a great cook, and it would be better for you.'

'If you say I need to stay indoors for a few more days I shall do something desperate,' he warned. 'You two mother hens are driving me crazy.'

'No, I was only going to say that anywhere else you'll get stared at. I'll come to Giant's Beacon.'

'You and Phantom.'

'He's included?'

'It wouldn't be the same without him. Friday evening.'

'I look forward to it. *We'll* look forward to it.'

He thanked her and departed. Outside the shop, he hesitated a moment, then headed for the harbour and the lifeboat station, but after a moment his attention was claimed by a man watching him from across the road with an air of nervousness. Enlightenment dawned, and he crossed over.

'I know you, don't I? You were part of the team that saved me from drowning.'

'I'm glad you remember that,' Walter said, 'and not the other thing.'

'You mean when you advised Harriet to let me drown?' Darius said, grinning.

'Ah, yes—'

'It's in the past,' Darius assured him. 'Look, do you have a moment? There's a pub over there.'

When they were settled with glasses of ale, Darius said, 'I want to show my gratitude in a practical way, with a donation to the lifeboat.' He took out his chequebook. 'Who do I make it out to?'

Walter told him, then looked, wide-eyed, at the amount. 'That's very generous.'

'It's not too much for my life. Will you make sure this reaches the right part of your organisation?'

'It'll be a pleasure. It's good to see you on your feet again. Harry said you were in a bad way.'

'All that time in the cold water. I reckon I was bound to go down with something. But Harriet got me home and took wonderful care of me.'

'She's a great girl, isn't she? Sometimes I wonder how she survived after what she's been through.'

'Been through?'

'Losing her husband. Oh, I know she's not the only widow in the world, but they had a fantastic marriage. Everyone who gets married hopes they're going to have what those two had. We all envied them. When he died we thought she might die too, she was so crushed. But she came back fighting. I don't reckon she'll ever really get over him, though.'

'But she's a young woman, with plenty of time to find someone else.'

'Yes, if she really wants to. But you only get something as good as that once in your life. It wouldn't surprise me if she stayed single now.' He drained his glass. 'Got to be going. Nice to meet you.'

They parted on good terms.

* * *

On Friday Darius came in the late afternoon to collect both his guests. Phantom leapt into the back seat of the car as though being chauffeured was no more than his right.

'Don't worry, I've washed him,' Harriet said.

Darius grinned over his shoulder at his four-pawed guest, who nuzzled his ear.

'Wait,' Harriet said suddenly, bouncing out of the car. 'I'll be back.'

He watched as she ran into her home, then out again a moment later, clutching a small black box.

'My pager,' she said, settling into the front seat. 'It has to go with me everywhere in case the lifeboat gets called out.'

'You're on call tonight?'

'Lifeboat volunteers are always on call. The only time that's not true is if we're ill, or have to leave the island for some reason. Then we give them notice of the dates and report back as soon as we return. But normally we take the pager everywhere and have to be ready to drop everything.'

'Everything? You mean…even if…suppose you were…?'

'At work or in the bath,' she supplied innocently. 'Yes, even then.'

That wasn't quite what he'd meant, and her mischievous look showed that she understood perfectly. For a moment another memory danced between them, when the edges of his robe had fallen open just long enough to be tantalising. By mutual consent they decided to leave it there.

'What made you want to be a lifeboat volunteer?' he asked as he started the car.

'My father. My mother died when I was very young and Dad raised me alone. When he went out on a call I used to love watching the boat go down the slipway into the water. All that spray coming up seemed so thrilling. He was a fisherman and I often went out with him. He taught me to be a sailor and bought me my first boat. My happiest times were spent on the water with him, and it was natural to follow him onto the lifeboats.'

'A fisherman? You mean herring?'

She laughed, 'Yes. There have always been shoals of herring in the water around here. Other fish too, but that's how the island got its name.'

'You've never wanted to leave it behind and move to the mainland?'

She made a face. 'Never! There's nowhere better in the world.'

'You sound very sure? As simple as that?'

'As simple as that. It's the best place on earth, and it always will be; unless something happens to spoil it.'

Darius didn't need to ask what she meant. He had the power to do the damage she mentioned, and they both knew it. But this wasn't the right moment.

The drive ran along the shoreline, from where they could see the sun beginning to set.

'I'd never seen anything like that before I came here,' he said.

'Never seen a sunset?'

'Not like a Herringdean sunset. I haven't been much by the sea. It's usually something I see looking down on from a plane.'

'Stop the car,' she urged.

He did as she asked and the three of them walked to the edge of the beach and stood watching as the water turned crimson, glittering as tiny waves broke softly. None of them made a sound. There was no need. Harriet glanced at Darius and saw on his face a look akin to the one she'd first seen when they met—absorbed, ecstatic. At last he gave a regretful sigh.

'We'd better go.'

'You can see it from the house,' she reassured him.

'In a way. But somehow it's different when you're out here with it.'

As they walked back to the car he glanced appreciatively at her appearance. Her soft blue dress wasn't expensive nor glamorous, but neither did it send out the warning he'd sensed from her functional bathing gear. Her light brown shoulder length hair flowed freely in soft waves. She looked relaxed and ready to enjoy herself and he found himself relaxing in turn.

The evening stretched ahead of him, warm and inviting. Another new experience. When had he last whiled away the hours with a friend?

Two friends, he realised, feeling Phantom nuzzle his hand.

'Just wait until we get home,' he said. 'Kate's got something really special for you.'

'I'm looking forward to it,' Harriet declared.

Man and dog stared at her, then at each other. Darius gave a shrug of resignation, and Harriet could almost have sworn that Phantom returned the gesture.

'You have to explain things carefully to women,' Darius told him.

Woof!

'You meant that remark about something special for Phantom?' Harriet demanded.

'Who else? Kate's taken a lot of trouble with his supper. I told her he was the guest of honour.'

Harriet chuckled. 'I guess you're learning.'

Kate was waiting at the door, beaming a welcome. For Phantom there was the dog equivalent of a banquet, which he tucked into with due appreciation. Her mind at ease, Harriet left him to it and followed Darius into the large dining room at the back where a table for two had been set up by the French windows. From here the lawn stretched out until it shaded into the stretch of private beach where they had first met.

'Remember?' he asked, filling her wine glass.

'I remember, and I shouldn't think you'll ever forget,' she said. 'You never did send me the bill for that suit.'

'Well, maybe I'm not the monster you think me to be,' he said.

'Thought, not think. I wouldn't dare think badly of someone who treats Phantom so well.'

'Ah, you've noticed that I'm grovelling to him. I'm so glad. I knew I had no chance of getting on your right side unless I got on his first.'

Harriet seemed to give this serious consideration. 'I see. And it's important to get on my right side?'

'Well, I can't let you go on being my enemy. It wouldn't be practical.'

'And at all costs we must be practical,' she agreed. 'But I have to say, Mr Falcon, that I'm disappointed at how badly you've misread the situation. I'd expected more efficiency from "the most fearsome man in London."'

'Please,' he protested. 'None of that. It was enough of an embarrassment when I could make a pretence of living up to it. Now—' He shuddered. 'But how did I misread the situation?'

'I was never your enemy.'

'Really? You expect me to believe that when you got a bodyguard for Phantom? Oh, yes, I heard. And then you despised me so much that you made jokes about leaving me to drown.'

'Well, you got your own back by walking in on me right after, didn't you? And I didn't leave you to drown—' She checked herself, alerted by his teasing look. 'Oh, ha ha! Well, I guess you're entitled to make fun of me.'

'Yes, I think I am as well,' he said, smiling and raising his glass. 'Truce?'

She regarded him with her head on one side. 'Armed?'

He nodded. 'Safer that way for both of us.'

'It's a deal.'

She raised her own glass and they clinked as Kate entered with the first dish.

'Just in time to save me from your terrible vengeance,' Darius said.

'Don't fool yourself,' she told him. 'When I wreak terrible vengeance on you, nothing and nobody will be able to save you.'

'Then I'd better have my supper quickly,' he said, leading her to the table.

Kate gave them a strange look and departed, making Harriet say in a quivering voice, trying not to laugh, 'She thinks we're both potty.'

'She's very observant.'

For a few moments they didn't speak, concentrating on the food, which was Kate's best, plain but delicious. Harriet wondered how it tasted to Darius, who must be used to more sophisticated fare, but he seemed happy to devour every mouthful.

'If I had "enemy" thoughts, so did you,' she observed. 'When you came upon us in the garden of the pub you seemed to hate me.'

She thought he wasn't going to reply, but then he nodded.

'I did. I heard you talking about how I looked on the beach, "standing there like a king come into his birthright" according to you.'

'That'll teach me to jump to conclusions,' she sighed. 'You weren't really feeling anything like that, were you?'

'No, I was feeling what a glorious place it was. It took me completely by surprise and I just stood there, stunned, trying to believe such beauty existed.'

'That was what I sensed when I first saw you,' she admitted. 'It was only later that I thought—oh, dear, I'm sorry. I guess I got it all wrong.'

'We both got a lot of things wrong, but this is the moment when we put it all behind us and become friends.'

'Friends…' She considered the word for a moment before saying, 'I must warn you, friends claim the right to ask each other questions.'

'Fire away.'

'Why did you go out to sea at all? It was madness.'

'I needed to see the wind farm, and learn all I could.'

'But surely you did an in-depth investigation before you bought the island?' Something in his wry expression made her say, 'You did, surely?'

'The first I heard about it was when Kate told me.'

She stared. 'I can't believe a smart operator like you bought this place without checking every detail first.'

He shrugged.

'You didn't?' she breathed. 'But why?'

'Perhaps I'm not quite as smart as I like people to think. Look, if I tell you, you've got to promise not to breathe a word to another soul.'

'I promise.'

'Seriously. Swear it on what you hold most dear.'

'I swear it on Phantom's life,' she said, holding up her hand. 'Now, tell, tell! The curiosity's driving me crazy.'

'I didn't buy Herringdean. Rancing owed me money, couldn't pay it, so he assigned the place to me, sent me the papers and vanished.'

'*What?*'

'My lawyer says everything's in order, I'm the legal

owner. But I had no chance to study the place, negotiate, refuse the deal, anything. Whatever I learn about the island comes as a surprise. My "investigation" consisted of looking Herringdean up online. What I found wasn't informative—fishing, beautiful countryside, but no mention of a wind farm.'

'Probably because it had only just got under way and they hadn't updated the site,' she mused.

'Exactly. So you see I've approached everything like a dimwit. All right, all right,' he added as she choked with laughter. 'Have your fun.'

'I'm sorry,' she gasped. 'I didn't mean to but—he fooled you—'

'Yes, he fooled me,' Darius said, managing to be faintly amused through his chagrin. 'And I'll tell you something else. Before he left, he got a lot of the bigger tenants to pay him several months' rent in advance, then he pocketed the money and ran. So it'll be a while before they pay me anything.'

He knew he was crazy to have told her such damaging things. If she betrayed his trust she could make him look like an idiot all over the island.

But she wouldn't betray him. Instinctively, he knew that he was safe with her.

Harriet was making confused gestures, trying to get her head around what she'd just heard.

'But the papers always say—you know, the mighty entrepreneur, all that stuff—'

'Been checking up on me, huh?' he said wryly.

'Of course. Be fair. Since you control our lives, I had to find out what I could.'

'Control your lives? Oh, sure, it looks like it. I arrive knowing nothing, nearly die finding out, get snatched from the jaws of death by you and the others. Some control! So I suppose you know all there is to know about me?'

Harriet shook her head. 'Only basics. Your father is Amos Falcon—*the* Amos Falcon. Empire builder, financial mogul—all right, all right.' She backed off hastily, seeing his expression. 'And you have lots of brothers. It must be nice coming from a large family. I'm an only child and it can be lonely.'

'So can being in a large family,' Darius said.

'Really? I can't imagine that. Tell me more.'

But suddenly his mouth closed in a firm line. It was as though something had brought him to the edge of a cliff, Harriet thought, and he'd backed away in alarm. She could almost see him retreating further and further.

'What is it?' she asked.

He rose and walked away to the window. She had a strange feeling that he was trying to put a distance between them, as though she was some kind of threat. After a moment's hesitation she followed him and laid a tentative hand on his arm.

'I'm sorry,' she said. 'Of course it's none of my business. I'm always sticking my nose into other people's affairs. Just ignore me.'

With anyone else he would have seized this offer with relief, but with her things were mysteriously different. In his mind he saw again the defining moment of their relationship, the moment when she had reached out to him, offering rescue, offering life. The moment had passed, yet it lived in him still and, he guessed, would always do so.

The need to accept her friendship, trust it, rely on it, was so strong that it sent warning signals. Nothing would ever be the same again. But there was no turning back now.

'I don't think I'll ignore you,' he said softly, taking her hand. 'You're not a woman that's easy to ignore.'

'I'll just vanish if you like.'

'No,' he said, his hand tightening on hers so suddenly that she gasped. 'Stay. I want you to stay.'

'All right,' she said. 'I'll stay.'

He led her back to the table and poured her a glass of wine.

'People always think big families are charming,' he said after a while. 'But it can be an illusion. Most of us didn't grow up together. My father's family was very poor and he had a hard life, which he was determined to escape at all costs. Some of the things he did don't look very sympathetic, but maybe if you have to live as he did—' He made an expressive gesture with his hands.

'Was he very—?' She paused delicately.

'Yes, very. Still is, for that matter. His family were miners, and he was expected to go down the pit. But his father had died down there and hell would freeze over before he went the same way. He did well at school, got top marks in practical subjects like maths. Not literature, or "the soft stuff" as he calls it. He reckons that's for fools. But with figures there's nothing he can't do.

'So he ran away and managed to start up his own business, just a little market stall, but it grew into a big one, and then bigger, until he got a shop.'

'He made enough profit to rent a shop? Wow!'

'Not rent. Buy. By that time he'd married my mother. She came from a rich family and they met when he made deliveries to their house. Her relatives did everything they could to stop the wedding. They believed all he really wanted was her money.'

'But they gave in at last?'

'No way. He simply ran off with her. "If you want something, go after it by the shortest route." That's his motto.

She gave him every penny she had. I know that because I've heard her father complaining about it.'

'But he probably loved her, and you. Surely everything in his life wasn't about money? It couldn't be, could it? There's always something else.'

'Is there?' he murmured. 'Is there?'

His face had changed. Now it wore a look of pain that made her take his hand in hers in a gesture of comfort.

'Don't say any more,' she said. 'Not if it hurts too much.'

He didn't answer. His gaze was fixed on the hand holding his, as it had once before. Then it had offered survival, now it offered another kind of life, one he couldn't describe. He had no talent for words, only figures. She'd spoken of it hurting him too much to talk, but now he knew that the real pain lay in not talking about things that had been shrouded in silence for too long. Somehow the words must come. But only with her.

CHAPTER FIVE

'I'LL tell you something,' Darius said at last. 'Falcon isn't my father's real name. He chose it for effect.'

'He wanted to be named after a bird?'

'No, he discovered that it has connections with a Roman consul and two princes.'

'You're kidding me.'

'Do you mean you've never heard of Pompeyo Falco?' Darius demanded with mock surprise. 'He was a very powerful Roman. The princes were Spanish, and there's even supposed to be a saint in the background. Not that he's ever made too much of that one. Nobody could keep a straight face.'

'I guess your father isn't much like a saint.'

'That's putting it mildly. He called me Darius because it means "wealthy". It was his way of signalling what he expected of me.'

Harriet dropped her face into her hands. 'I can hardly believe it,' she said at last. 'It's like something out of a mad fantasy.'

'That's just what it is. I grew up knowing what I had to do to please my father—or else! Luckily, I'd inherited his head for figures, so I was able to live up to at least some of his expectations.'

'Only some?'

'He's not pleased with me at the moment, losing so much money and letting things crumble under me.'

'But that's happened to a lot of people.'

'Doesn't matter. It shouldn't have happened to a Falcon. He's currently considering whether I, or one of my brothers, does him the most credit. At the moment I think I'm bottom of the list.'

Harriet frowned. 'I think I read somewhere that your brothers come from different parts of the world,' she said carefully.

'If you mean that my father spread himself thinly, yes, that's right. As the business built up he did a lot of travelling, first in England, then abroad. I don't think he was ever faithful to my mother for five minutes; that's how, in addition to a full brother, I come to have a half-brother from Russia, one from France, and one from America.

'In the end my mother couldn't stand it any more and she left, taking my brother Jackson and me with her. But she died after a few years and my father reclaimed us. By that time he had a new wife and a new son. We entered their house as strangers, and that was how we felt for a long time. Jackson coped better, although even he had a tough time with our stepmother.'

'She was furious that we were there at all because that meant that her boy, Marcel, wasn't the eldest. When she caught my father playing around she left him and went back to France. Marcel turned up a few years ago and, oddly enough, we all get on well. Our father has helped him start up in business in Paris, and I understand he's a real chip off the old block.'

'More than you?' she asked shrewdly.

He hesitated before saying, 'Who can say?'

Greatly daring, she ventured to ask, 'Is that what you want? To be like him?'

'I don't know,' he said. 'It's all become confused. When I was growing up my one thought was to follow in his footsteps and be a power in the land. People were awed by him, they hurried to please him, and that seemed wonderful to me. But I was immature and, as you grow up, things happen to you—'

He grew silent. After a while he repeated softly, 'I simply don't know.'

A noise made him look up quickly, smiling as if everything was normal. Nobody, Harriet thought, could guess that the moment of insight had taken him by surprise. Now she felt he was trying to forget it.

'Ah, here's Kate with the next course,' he said cheerfully. 'And not only Kate.'

Phantom had slipped in and came to curl up near the table.

'Have you had enough?' Harriet asked, caressing his ears. 'Has the guest of honour been properly cared for?'

A soft woof was the reply.

'How did Phantom happen to be with you and the rest of the crew that night?' Darius asked when they were alone again. 'I gather you'd been out on a shout. Don't tell me he comes too?'

She laughed. 'No, I left him with my neighbour—'

'To protect him from me?'

'Please.'

'All right, I won't say it again.'

'She was out walking him when she saw the boat coming home across the water, so she waited, then came and joined us.'

'How old is he?'

'Fourteen, maybe. He belonged to Brad, my husband, before we married, and he'd got him from a home for abandoned dogs, so he wasn't sure of his age. I know he's getting on a bit but he's still full of beans.'

There was a hint of defiance in her voice that warned Darius to go carefully. Fourteen was old for a dog, especially a large one, but not for the world would he have voiced his conviction that she would soon lose her beloved companion.

'Talking of being full of beans, are you really better?' she asked.

'I'm fine now. I've spent some time in bed—why that cynical look?'

'I'm getting to understand you now. All that time in bed, I'll bet you weren't alone.'

'No, I haven't seduced any willing ladies—'

'I meant you had your laptop computer with you.'

'Ah…yes…I see.' He met her teasing eyes and grinned sheepishly. 'I fell right into that one, didn't I? Yes, I did have it with me now and then. But not always. I got a lot of sleep and I have to admit you and Kate were right. It was what I needed. And, as well as rest, I've been taking exercise. I go swimming from my private beach. I keep looking out for you, but you're never there.'

Her eyes widened in theatrical innocence. 'But how can I be? I don't have the permission of the owner. He's a terrible man. When he found me there once before he was very annoyed.'

'No, you just imagined that.' He grinned. 'In future you go there whenever you like. And take Phantom too.'

A soft noise from under the table told him that this was appreciated.

'And I'm not glued to the computer all the time,' he continued.

'No, I'm sure you read the *Financial Times* and *The Wall Street Journal*—'

'I've been reading up about Herringdean and its history. It's fascinating.'

'You'll find that this island is two places,' she said. 'We're not behind the times. There's plenty of dot-com. But it's the wildness that makes Herringdean stand out, and draws people.'

'Have you always lived on the island?'

'Yes, I was born here.'

'And your husband?'

'No, he came over because he worked for a tourist firm, and they were setting up a branch.'

'And you met, fell in love and married quickly?'

'A couple of months.'

'Wow! A decisive lady! How long were you married?'

'Nearly eight years.'

'Any children?'

'No,' she said quietly.

'And he died quite recently?'

'Last year.' Suddenly she became animated. 'You know, this coffee is really delicious. Kate is a wonderful cook.'

He was silent. Walter was there in his mind, talking about Harriet's husband, saying, 'When he died we thought she might die too, she was so crushed…I don't reckon she'll ever really get over him…'

Now the way she'd swerved off the subject seemed to suggest that Walter was right. It was a warning to him to be cautious.

'What about your children?' Harriet asked. 'Have you managed to call them again?'

'Yes, several times. There's a dangerous situation building up. Mary's going to remarry soon, and if I'm not careful I could be elbowed aside.'

'But you won't let that happen.'

'No, I won't. I had time to do a lot of thinking while

I was resting. It's incredible how being half-awake, half-asleep can make things clear to you.'

Harriet nodded, and for a moment there was a faraway look in her eyes that roused his curiosity. But it vanished before he could speak, and now he thought he understood. Beneath her cheeky schoolgirl charm lurked a woman who kept her true feelings, and even her true self, safely hidden away. In fact, she was mysteriously like himself.

'So what conclusions have you come to?' she asked.

'Not to let myself be sidelined. I try to call them every day.'

'I'm sure they're glad of that.'

He made a face. 'They're not. I made a hash of it the night of the accident and things haven't really improved.'

'Well, you weren't at ease on the phone, I could hear that, but surely they understood what a state you were in.'

'Maybe, but I'm seldom much better than I was then. I don't know what to talk about. It was easier when we were living in the same house, but I'm not really part of their lives any more. Perhaps I never really was. Mary accused me of never putting them first.'

She nodded. 'Children really do like to feel that they have all your attention,' she mused.

Suddenly he saw her as she'd been that day in the shop, talking to the little boy as though only he existed in the entire world. And the child had responded with delight. When had he seen such a look on the faces of his own children?

'You've got a fight on your hands,' she said, 'but you've got to go about it the right way. Do you want some advice from a friend?'

'If the friend is you, yes.'

'That night when you called them after the accident I heard her voice on the other end. I couldn't make out every word but I heard enough to show me an unhappy situation. You told her you'd been "held up" and she said, "You always get held up. The children went to bed crying because you didn't keep your word."

'And then she said, "I'm not going to let you hurt them by putting them last again."'

She waited to see if he would say anything, but he only clasped his hands on the table and stared at them.

'Again?' she asked.

'Yes, I can't deny it. I would plan to spend time with them, but a crisis would come up, someone I urgently needed to meet would be passing through London for just a few hours.'

'Oh, you idiot!' she breathed.

'I guess I am, but I didn't see it then. I always thought there was time to put things right.'

'Yes, we always think that,' she murmured. 'There never is.'

'You sound as though you really know.'

'I guess we all know one way or another.'

'Sure, but the way you said it sounded as though—'

'The thing is—' she interrupted him quickly '—that you have to find a new way to put things right. Concentrate on that.'

'All right,' he said, retreating before the warning she was sending out. 'But how? One minute I thought I was in control. The next minute they were all gone, and if I was a hopeless father before I'm even worse now. When we talk on the phone I can sense them trying to get away. I'm becoming an irrelevance to them.'

'Then do something about it,' she said urgently. 'Put a stop to it now. Never forget that cunning is better than aggression. Above all, don't lose heart, don't even think of giving in. Remember, you're a match for anyone.'

'If you're going to start on that "mighty man of business" stuff again I'm out of here.'

'Don't worry,' she said wryly. 'I can't take it seriously any more.'

'Thanks. That about says it all.'

'Friends have to be frank with each other,' she reminded him.

'I know.' He suddenly became more urgent. 'Harriet, I wish I could make you understand how much I need your friendship. From the moment I stepped onto that beach I knew I was in a different world, and now I know that it's your world. All the vital things that have happened to me since I came here are connected with you.'

'You never know what fate has in store.'

'Yes, after we got off to such a bad start, who could have guessed that you'd be the one who'd save me?'

'Be fair. It was Kate who really saved you, not just by raising the alarm, but by explaining that you'd probably gone to the wind farm, so that we knew where to look.'

'I know that, and I've shown her my gratitude.'

Harriet nodded. Kate had told her about the huge bonus he'd given her.

'And I didn't pull you out of the water on my own. There were a few hefty fellers there, doing the heavy work.'

'I know. But yours was the hand that stretched out to me first, the hand that I clasped, and when I think of that moment that's what I see.'

It was also what he felt in the night, feeling a firm, reassuring grip on his hand, knowing it was her in the last moment before he awoke to find himself alone. Only a dream, yet his hand still seemed to tingle.

'I've just become a sort of symbol, that's all,' she told him.

'If you say so.'

'But if you want a friend, you've got one in me.'

'Promise?'

'Promise. Call on me any time.'

As long as you're here, she thought. But how long will that be? Are we a financial asset to you, or a financial disaster? And won't it be the same in the long run?

It would have been sensible to say this outright and remind him of the reality of the situation, yet something held her silent. There was an intensity in his eyes that she'd never seen before in any man—not the passionate intensity of a lover, but the desperate yearning for help of a man who needed friendship. It had been her hand he'd first seized in the water and that had set matters between them for all time.

'You may regret saying that,' he said. 'I'll call on you more often than you think.'

'I'll never regret saying it. I'm here for you.'

'Shake on it?'

She took the hand he offered, and felt her own hand engulfed. She could sense the power, as she'd sensed it that other time when he'd held her against her will to study her face. But now she also felt the gentleness deep within him, knowing instinctively that few people were ever allowed to know about it.

He touched her heart—not as a lover, she assured herself. That part of her life had died a year ago. But his need spoke to her, making it impossible for her to turn her back on him.

'Shake,' she said.

A couple of days later she resumed bathing on his beach. After splashing around with Phantom for half an hour she gasped, 'All right, boy. Time we were going.'

But as she turned towards the shore she was halted by

the sight of Darius, striding onto the beach wearing a dark blue towel bathrobe, which he stripped off, showing his black bathing gear beneath.

Instead of tight-fitting trunks he wore shorts, looser and less revealing, leaving many of her questions still unanswered. Even so, she could see that he was more powerfully built than a mere businessman had any right to be. If there was any justice in the world he would be scrawny, not taut and lean, with long muscular arms and legs.

He saw her and waved. Next moment he was running into the water and powering towards her. She laughed and swam away, swerving this way and that until he caught up, reaching out his hands. She seized them and he immediately began to back-pedal, drawing her with him. As they reached the shore she slipped away, laughing, and he chased her up the beach to where he'd dropped his bathrobe next to her towel.

Phantom galloped after them, delighted at the prospect of a rematch, but this time Darius was ready for him, dropping to one knee, greeting his 'opponent' with outstretched arms and rolling on the sand with him.

'I reckon that's about even,' he said, getting up at last.

'Now you really are a mess,' she said, regarding the sand that covered him.

'Yes, I am, aren't I?' he agreed with something that sounded suspiciously like satisfaction. 'All right, play's over. Time for the serious stuff. See you tomorrow.'

So it went on for several days—pleasant, undemanding friendship with almost the innocence of childhood. It seemed strange to think of this man in such a light, but when she saw him fooling with Phantom it was hard to remember his harsh reputation, and the power he held over them all.

Then he vanished.

'He just took off without a word,' Kate said when they bumped into each other while shopping. 'He was sitting at the computer when I took in his morning coffee. I don't know what he saw there but it made him say a very rude word. Then he made a phone call. I got out fast but I could hear a lot more rude words.'

Walter, who also happened to be there, said, 'Only rude words?'

'I heard him say, "I don't care; it mustn't be allowed to happen," and "Do you realise what this would mean if—?" and "When I get my hands on him I'll—" and then more rude words.'

'Sounds like a disaster,' Walter observed.

'Nah,' Kate said. 'Not him. He's too big for disaster. You mark my words, they can't touch him.'

'That's not what the papers say,' Walter insisted. 'This "credit crunch" thing has hit all the big shots. Next thing you know he'll have to sell this place and we'll have someone new to worry about.'

'Oh, stop panicking!' Harriet said, trying to sound amused and not quite succeeding. 'He's better than Rancing. The furniture shops love him now he's started kitting out Giant's Beacon, and he's given quite a bit to charity.'

'Yes, I heard about that donation to the animal shelter,' Walter said. 'I wondered how he knew about it—unless you told him.'

'I may have mentioned it. He likes to be told about things.'

'Yes, everyone's talking about how you and he swim together in the mornings. You're a clever lass, getting on his right side.' He added significantly, 'You probably know more than anyone.'

'I know he looks fantastic in swimming gear,' she agreed.

'That's not what I meant.'

Yes, she thought, she knew what he meant. This was the moment a less loyal friend would tell how he'd been tricked by Rancing, exposing him to ridicule. For the first time she appreciated how vulnerable Darius had left himself by confiding in her.

'We don't discuss business,' she said. 'I wouldn't understand it if we did. I've no idea where he's gone, why he's gone or when he'll be back.'

Or if he'll ever be back, she thought sadly.

She didn't doubt that another financial calamity had befallen him, and that he'd gone to try to head off trouble. It must be urgent because, despite their friendship, he hadn't left her a word. Still she was sure he would call her.

But he didn't. Days passed without a word. Wryly, she decided that this was a lesson in reality. When his real world called she simply ceased to exist, that was something to remember in the future.

If there was a future.

Harriet tried to follow the financial news and learned of the sudden collapse of a property company with global tentacles, but she could only guess whether he had had an interest there.

Then, just when she'd decided that he'd gone for good, Darius turned her world upside down yet again. As she and Phantom headed for their morning swim he suddenly gave a bark of joy and charged onto the beach to where a figure lay stretched out on the sand. Fending off the dog, who was trying to lick him to death, Darius rose on one elbow and watched her approach.

'Hello, stranger,' she said when she could speak through her emotion.

'I hoped you'd be here,' he said as she dropped beside him. 'I got back at three in the morning and came out here so as not to miss you. I dozed off for a while, but I knew someone would wake me. All right, Phantom, cool it, there's a good fellow.'

'Did things go as you'd hoped?' she asked.

'More or less. I averted disaster—until next time.'

'You mean we're safe—here on the island?'

'You're safe. This is the last place in the world that I'd give up. Now, I need to ask a huge favour from you, an act of friendship. It's very important to me.'

'Then consider it done.'

'I told you Mary left me for another man, and they were planning marriage. Well, the date has been set, and I've been invited.'

'To your ex-wife's wedding?'

'Yes, it took a bit of manoeuvring, but I managed it. I told her we should seem friendly for the sake of the children. They'll be there so we'll get some time together and they'll know their parents are on good terms. You see, I really took your advice.'

'*I* advised this?'

'You said cunning was better than aggression, and it took all my cunning to manipulate myself an invitation. Mary finished by saying she completely agreed with me and she praised me for thinking of it. She even said I must be improving.' He gave a self-deprecating grin. 'And I owe it all to you.'

He spread his hands in a gesture of finality, his expression radiating such cheerful triumph that she chuckled and said, 'You're telling me that *I* instructed *you* in cunning?'

'There's cunning and cunning,' he said. 'Some kinds I'm better at than others. Manipulating share prices is easy, but—'

'But a child's heart is more complicated than a share price,' she supplied.

'You see how right I was to listen to you. The best friend and adviser I have.'

'Stop buttering me up,' she said severely, 'and tell me what you want me to do.'

'Come with me to the wedding, of course. How can I turn up alone when my ex-wife is marrying another guy? I'd look like a prat.'

'And we can't have that,' she said in mock horror. 'If the markets got to hear—'

'All right, make fun of me. I wouldn't put up with it from anyone else, but with you I guess it's the price of friendship. OK, I'll pay it.

'And there's another thing. I told you about my father and how he likes to control everyone's life. His latest mad idea is to marry me off to Freya, my stepsister. Either me or one of my brothers, but at the moment it's my head he's trying to put on the block.

'Luckily, Freya's no more keen than I am. We get on all right, but that's all. If I can convince my father that it's not going to happen then he'll turn his attention to one of the others.'

'Poor Freya.'

'That's what I think. You'll like her.'

'But will she be at the wedding? And your father? Isn't he furious with Mary for leaving you?'

'Yes, he is. He's even more furious because she managed to get a decent divorce settlement out of me, but he'll want to see his grandchildren. They're Falcons, which means that in his mind they're his property. He doesn't have much contact with them because they live in London and he can't leave Monte Carlo very often.'

'For tax reasons?' she hazarded.

'That's right. He's only allowed to be in England for ninety-one days. Any more and he'd be counted as an

English resident and liable for English tax. He's nearly used up his allowance for this year so he has to dash to London for the wedding, and get back very quickly.'

How casually he spoke, she realised. How normal he seemed to consider this. It was a reminder that his life was centred around money, just in case she was in danger of forgetting.

'And your brothers?' she asked. 'Will they be there?'

'As many as can manage it. They all like Mary, rather more than they like me, actually. And the kids are fascinated by them coming from so many different countries. To them it's like a circus. So we're all going to bury our differences, but you won't send me into the lion's den alone, will you?'

Harriet regarded him sardonically. 'You really don't feel you can face it without me?'

'Definitely not. I'm shaking in my shoes at the prospect.'

There it was in his eyes, the teasing humour that linked with her own mind in a contact sweeter than she had ever known.

'In that case, I'll just have to come along and protect you,' she sighed. 'It's a dreadful responsibility, but I guess I'll manage.'

'I knew you wouldn't fail me. The wedding's in London in two weeks' time. It'll be a civil ceremony held at the Gloriana Hotel, and that's where the reception will be too, so I'll book us in there. You'll be my guest, of course, but we'll have separate rooms, so don't worry. Every propriety will be observed.'

Propriety. There was that word again. How often it cropped up in her mind with regard to this man, always implying the opposite.

Don't go, said a warning voice in her mind. *To him this is a matter of friendship, but can you keep it as mere friendship? You don't even know the answer, and oh, how you wish you did! Stay here, keep yourself safe.*

'I'd love to come,' she said.

CHAPTER SIX

OVER the next few days Harriet made her preparations, arranging extra hours for her assistant, notifying the lifeboat station that she would be away so that they could arrange a substitute to be on call. Her neighbour would look after Phantom, and she explained her coming absence to him with many caresses. He accepted these politely but seemed far more interested in the box of bones that had been delivered from Giant's Beacon.

On the last day before their departure Harriet and Darius went for a final swim, frolicking like children, splashing each other, laughing fit to bust.

Harriet knew that at the back of her mind there was an unfamiliar aspect to her happiness. Part of her had been so sure that their friendship was over, but then he'd drawn her back in, seeking her help and her warmth again, and it was like a balm to her spirit. Suddenly all she wanted to do was laugh and dance.

As they raced up the beach she stopped suddenly and looked around.

'My towel's vanished. Where—? *Phantom.*'

In the distance they could see him tearing along the sand, her towel in his jaws, deaf to her cries.

'He'll be back in his own good time,' Darius said.

'But what do I do in the meantime?'

'Let me dry you.' In a moment he'd flung his towel around her, drawing it close in front, and began to rub her down. She shrieked with laughter and tried to wriggle away but he held her a prisoner while his hands moved over her.

'You wretch,' she cried, pummelling him. 'Let me go.'

But it was no use. He had ten times her strength, as she was beginning to understand. And there was something else she understood. She'd been mad to engage in this struggle that drew her near-naked body so close to his. The pleasure that was pervading her now was more than laughter with a dear friend. His flesh against hers, his face close to her own, the meeting of their eyes; she should have avoided these things like the plague. Except that he hadn't given her the chance.

Caution, she'd promised herself, but where was caution now? And did she really care?

'Let me go,' she repeated.

But now his arms had enfolded her completely, allowing no movement.

'Make me,' he challenged.

She made a half-hearted attempt to kick him but only ended up with her leg trapped between his.

'Do you call that making me?' he demanded.

'Will you stop this?'

'Nope.'

It shocked her to realise how disappointed she would have been if his answer had been any different.

'What do you think you're doing?' she cried.

'I just thought it was time you learned who was boss around here.'

'OK, you're boss. Now let me go.'

'Only if you pay the ransom.'

'And what's that?'

'This,' he said, dropping his head.

It wasn't a major kiss, no big deal, she told herself, trying not to respond to the gentle pressure of his lips. But it was precisely that light touch that was her undoing, making her want to lean forward, demanding that he kiss her more deeply, and more deeply still, threatening her with her own desires. And with that threat came fear.

'No,' she whispered. 'No.'

'I wonder if you really mean that.'

She too wondered, but now she gathered all her strength together and said more firmly, *'No!'*

He drew back a little, frowning.

'You promised this wouldn't happen,' she reminded him.

'I didn't exactly—'

'Every propriety observed, you said.'

'Does that mean I can't even kiss you?'

'It means you can't kiss me now, just when we're about to embark on this idea of yours, pretending to be together when we aren't really.'

Slowly he released her and she took the chance to step back.

'Isn't this something we have to work out as we go along?' he asked.

'You're a businessman, Darius. I'm sure you know that when exploring new territory it's wise to have a plan.'

'And is that your plan?' he demanded. 'To turn away from all human desire?'

'*I have to.* Can't you try to understand? I'm not sure that I can ever…I don't know, *I don't know.*'

'But how long? For the rest of your life? Was he really that perfect?'

She took a step back and her face was distraught. 'Leave me alone. Just leave me alone.'

He sighed. 'Yes, all right. I'm sorry, Harriet. I should have known better. You have to pick your own time. I can't pick it for you. I shouldn't have—it's just that I've wanted to do that for some time and…well, I guess you don't want to know that.'

'I'd rather not,' she agreed.

'Just try to forgive me, please.'

'There's nothing to forgive,' she said calmly. 'It didn't happen. Now, I think it's time we went and started to get ready. We have a long day tomorrow.'

Harriet left him without a backward glance, followed by Phantom, dragging her towel.

After a moment Darius walked after them, cursing himself for clumsiness.

The trip to London was like nothing Harriet had ever known before. Darius had chartered a helicopter that collected them from the lawn and swept them up and over the channel. Looking down, she drew in her breath.

'Herringdean looks so different, and the sea—nothing is the way I know it below.'

'Yes, they're different worlds,' he agreed, looking down with her. 'And it can be hard to know which one is the place you belong.'

'I suppose it wouldn't be possible to belong in the world up here,' she said thoughtfully. 'You could never stay up that long.'

'True. Sooner or later you have to come down to earth,' he said in a voice that had a touch of regret.

In London, they landed at an airport where a car was waiting, ready to sweep them into the West End, the place of theatres, expensive shops and even more expensive hotels.

The sight of the Gloriana Hotel rearing up eight floors

startled Harriet. She'd guessed that it would be luxurious, but the reality took her by surprise. Again, she wondered if she'd been wise to come here, but it was too late. The chauffeur was carrying their bags to the door. Darius had drawn her arm through his and for his sake she must steel herself. He'd asked this as an act of friendship—and from now on she had only one function; to do him credit so that he could hold up his head.

It needed all her resolution when she saw the inside of the hotel with its marble floor and columns. As Darius had promised, they had separate accommodation but they were next door to each other. When he'd left her alone she studied her surroundings. The bedroom was the largest she had ever seen, and the bathroom was an elegant dream of white porcelain and silver taps. She knew she should have been in heaven, but such luxury intimidated her even more.

Ah, well, she thought resolutely. Best dress forward!

But unpacking was a dismal experience. Suddenly none of her dresses seemed 'best' as it would be understood in the Gloriana.

Then she recalled seeing a gown shop in the reception area. A moment to check that she'd brought her credit cards and she was out of the door, hurrying to the elevator.

The shop exceeded her wildest expectations. The clothes were glorious. So, too, were the prices but she decided to worry about that later. Anything was better than looking like a little brown mouse in the kind of elegant company that Darius regarded as normal.

Two dresses held her undecided for a while, but at last—

'I'll take this one,' she said.

'And the other one,' said Darius's voice behind her. 'They both suit you.'

She whirled to face him. 'How did you—?'

'When I found your room empty I asked the desk and they told me you were here. You should have brought me with you so we could make the decision together. Mind you, I like your choices.' To the assistant he said, 'We'll take both of these, please.'

'No,' she muttered urgently. 'I can't afford them both.'

'You?' He regarded her with quizzically raised eyebrows. 'What has this got to do with you?'

'Evidently, nothing,' she said.

'I invited you here to do me a favour. I don't expect you to buy your own clothes as well.'

Light dawned.

'When you say clothes you mean props, don't you? I'm playing a part and the director chooses the costumes?'

'Got it in one.'

'Next thing, you'll be telling me I'm tax deductible.'

'Now there's a thought! Come on, let's get to work. What have you chosen for the wedding?'

'I thought that one,' she said, indicating her first choice.

'No, something a little more formal.' He turned away to murmur to the assistant, and another flow of gowns was produced.

'Try that on,' Darius said, pointing to a matching dress and jacket.

Turning this way and that before the mirror, she saw it looked stunning on her. As Darius said, it was only right that he should pay the expenses, and when would she get the chance to dress like this again? She fought temptation for the briefest moment before yielding happily. It would take more stern virtue than she could manage to reject this.

While the dress was being packed up Darius said, 'Now, about jewellery.' As if anticipating her protest, he hurried on, 'I'm afraid this will only be hired. Take a look at these.'

If they hadn't been on hire she knew she couldn't have accepted the gold, silver and diamonds that were displayed before her. As it was, she was able to make her choice with a clear conscience.

Before they returned to their rooms Darius led her to the back of the hotel, where a huge ballroom was being decorated.

'This is where they'll hold the party tonight,' he said. 'And tomorrow night the wedding reception will be here.'

More size. This place had been created to hold a thousand. So why was she on edge? she wondered. She was at ease with the much greater size of the ocean. But that was natural, not created artificially to be impressive and profitable. She could never be at ease in an environment like this.

But she smiled, said the right things and tried to look as if she belonged here.

'I've got to go and make phone calls,' Darius said as they reached her room. 'I'll have something delivered for you to eat, then why don't you put your feet up until your attendants get here?'

'Attendants?'

'Hairstyle, make-up. Just leave it to them. You don't need to worry about a thing.'

In other words, she thought, let them array her in her stage costume and make her up for the performance.

'All right,' she said good-humouredly. 'I promise not to interfere with my own appearance.'

'That's my girl! Bye.'

He dropped the briefest kiss on her cheek and was gone, leaving Harriet alone and thoughtful. A mirror on the wall of the corridor showed her a neat, efficient young woman, pleasant but not dynamic.

Still, I've never had much chance to be dynamic, she thought. *And who knows—?*

Her reflection challenged her, sending the message, *Don't kid yourself.*

But why not? she thought. *If I want to kid myself, that's my business. Hey, I forgot to ask him—*

Approaching his door, she raised her hand to knock, then stopped as she heard Darius's voice.

'Mary? So you've arrived at last. Are the kids with you?—Fine, I'm on my way.'

Harriet heard the phone being replaced, and moved fast. By the time Darius emerged, the corridor was empty.

Lying on the bed, she tried to rest as Darius had advised, but her mind was too full of questions. What was happening now between him and his ex-wife, between him and his children? Would the wedding be dramatically called off at the last minute because of a reconciliation?

And why should she care? She'd had her chance and turned it down.

The chance wouldn't come again. She must force herself to remember that.

But after only half an hour she heard him return, walking quickly along the corridor until he entered his room and slammed the door like a man who was really annoyed.

After that she dozed until there was a knock at her door.

Even though Darius had told her about the attendants, what happened next was a shock. They simply took her over, allowing no room for argument, and proceeded to turn her into someone else. She yielded chiefly out of curiosity. She was fascinated to discover her new self.

If she'd been fanciful—which she prided herself on never

being—she might have thought of Cinderella. The fairy godmother, or godmothers since there were two of them, waved their wands and the skivvy was transformed into a princess.

Or at least a passable imitation of one, she thought. How well she could carry it off was yet to be seen.

When she was alone again she surveyed herself in the mirror, wondering who was this glamorous creature with the elegant swept-up hair, wearing the dark red glittering cocktail dress. She had always regarded herself as a tad too thin, but only a woman with her shape could have dared to wear this tight-fitting gown that left no doubt about her tiny waist and long legs, while revealing her bosom as slightly fuller than she had imagined.

A princess, she thought. Princess Harry? Not sure about that.

Even she, self-critical though she was, could see how the expert make-up emphasised the size of her blue eyes, which seemed to have acquired a new sparkle, and the width of her shapely mouth.

From nowhere came the memory of her husband, whose work in tourism had often taken him away on trips.

'I could get jealous of all those expensively dressed women you meet,' she'd teased him once.

'Forget it,' he'd told her. 'You don't need that fancy stuff. You're better as you are.'

'A country bumpkin?' she'd chuckled.

'*My* country bumpkin,' he'd insisted, silencing her in the traditional way, making her so happy that she'd believed him and wasn't jealous. Only to discover at last that she should have been.

And if he'd ever seen her looking like this? Would anything have been different?

Suddenly she wanted very badly to find Darius, see the

expression in his eyes when he first glimpsed her. Then she would know—

Know what?

If she only knew that, she would know everything. And it was time to find out.

A few moments later, she was knocking on Darius's door. As soon as he opened it he grew still. Then he nodded slowly.

'Yes,' he said. *'Yes.'*

'Will I do?'

'You cheeky little devil; I've already given you the answer to that.'

He drew her into the room and stood back to look at her, then made a twirling movement with his hand. She turned slowly, giving him time to appreciate every detail, then back again, displaying herself to full advantage. After all, she reasoned, he was entitled to know that his money had been well spent.

'As long as I do you credit.'

'I'll be the envy of every man there.'

And that, she thought, was what he chiefly cared about, apart from his children. She was there to be useful, and it would be wise to remember that. But it was hard when the excitement was growing in her.

Darius put his hands on her shoulders, holding her just a few inches away, his eyes fixed on her face.

'Beautiful,' he said. 'Just as I hoped. Just as I imagined. Just as—'

'Am I interrupting anything?' said a voice from the doorway.

Darius beamed at the young man standing there. 'Marcel!' he exclaimed.

Next moment, he was embracing the newcomer, thumping him on the back and being thumped in return.

Marcel, Harriet thought. The half brother from Paris.

'I'm sorry to come in without knocking,' he said, 'but the door was open.'

His eyes fell on Harriet, and the pleasurable shock in them was very satisfying.

'You've been keeping this lady a big secret,' he said, speaking with the barest trace of a French accent. 'And I understand why. If she were mine I would also hide her away from the world. Introduce me. I insist.'

'This is Harriet,' Darius replied, moving beside her.

'Harriet,' Marcel echoed. 'Harriet. It is a beautiful name.'

She couldn't resist saying cheekily, 'Actually, my friends call me Harry.'

'*Harry?*' He seemed aghast, muttering something in French that might have been a curse. 'That is a monstrosity, to give a man's name to such a beautiful lady. And this fellow allows them to treat you like this? You should be rid of him at once.'

'Cut it out!' Darius said, grinning, which seemed to amuse Marcel even more.

'Just thought I'd get in the mood now the circus has come to town,' he said.

'Circus is right,' Darius agreed. 'I've warned Harriet.'

'Harriet? You mean *you* don't call her Harry? But of course, you're not a friend; you are—' He made a vague but significant gesture.

'Hey,' she said and he turned his merry gaze on her. 'Don't jump to conclusions,' she told him impishly.

'Ah, yes, I see. How wise.'

'Can we drop this?' Darius asked.

'Certainly. So, Harriet, Darius has warned you, and you know we're a load of oddities.'

'I'll bet you're no odder than me,' she riposted.

GET FREE BOOKS and FREE GIFTS WHEN YOU PLAY THE...

Lucky 7

Just scratch off the silver box. Then check below to see the gifts you get!

SLOT MACHINE GAME!

YES!

I have scratched off the silver box. Please send me the 2 free Harlequin® Romance books and 2 free gifts for which I qualify. I understand I am under no obligation to purchase any books, as explained on the back of this card.

❏ I prefer the regular-print edition
116/316 HDL FEFN

❏ I prefer the larger-print edition
186/386 HDL FEFN

FIRST NAME   LAST NAME

ADDRESS

APT.#   CITY

STATE/PROV.   ZIP/POSTAL CODE

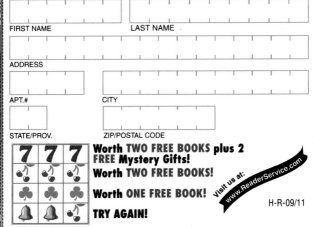

7 7 7	**Worth TWO FREE BOOKS plus 2 FREE Mystery Gifts!**
🍒🍒🍒	**Worth TWO FREE BOOKS!**
♣♣♣	**Worth ONE FREE BOOK!**
🔔🔔🍒	**TRY AGAIN!**

Visit us at: www.ReaderService.com

H-R-09/11

DETACH AND MAIL CARD TODAY!

H-R-09/11

The Reader Service—Here's How It Works:

If offer card is missing write to: The Reader Service, P.O. Box 1867, Buffalo NY 14240-1867 or visit www.ReaderService.com

BUSINESS REPLY MAIL
FIRST-CLASS MAIL   PERMIT NO. 717   BUFFALO, NY

POSTAGE WILL BE PAID BY ADDRESSEE

THE READER SERVICE
PO BOX 1867
BUFFALO NY 14240-9952

NO POSTAGE
NECESSARY
IF MAILED
IN THE
UNITED STATES

'I'll take you up on that. Promise me a dance tonight.'

'She declines,' Darius said firmly.

'Oh, do I?'

'Definitely.'

Marcel chuckled and murmured in Harriet's ear, 'We'll meet again later.'

'Are any of the others here?' Darius asked.

'Jackson. Travis isn't coming. He can't leave America—some television series he's working on. Leonid tried to get here but an urgent meeting came up at the last minute. And our honourable father arrived an hour ago, but I expect you already know that.'

'No, he hasn't been in touch. I'm in his black books at the moment. Anyone with him?'

'Janine and Freya.'

Harriet's teasing impulse got the better of her again and made her say, 'Ah, yes, she's the one you're supposed to be marrying, isn't she?'

'You can stop that kind of talk,' Darius said, while Marcel grinned.

'A lady with a sense of humour,' he said. 'That's what I like. Believe me, you're going to need it. I said before that it was a circus, and Papa is the ringmaster. He cracks the whip and we jump through hoops—or at least we pretend to.'

'Yes,' Darius growled.

'I gather you're not playing his game,' Marcel said, his eyes on Harriet again.

'Right, and so I've told him. Let's hope he believes me.'

'You realise that means he'll set his sights on Jackson or me next,' Marcel complained. 'Luckily, Freya finds me irritating.'

Darius grinned. 'I can't think why.'

'Neither can I. Right, I'll be off. I'll see you at the reception.'

He blew Harriet a kiss and hurried away.

'I like your brother,' she said when the door had closed.

'Most women do,' Darius observed wryly.

'No, I mean he looks fun.'

'Most women say that too.'

'Which is why you find him irritating?'

'He's a good fellow. We get on most of the time. It may have crossed my mind that he sometimes has it too easy in certain areas. Mary used to accuse me of being jealous of his charm, and perhaps she was right. Charm isn't one of my virtues.' He gave her a wry look. 'As you've found out.'

As he spoke he reached for her hand, and some impulse made her enfold his in both of hers, squeezing comfortingly.

'Charm isn't always a virtue,' she said. 'A man can have too much of it.'

'Well, nobody's ever accused me of that.'

'Good. Just honesty—'

'I hope so.'

'And upright virtue.'

'Nobody's ever accused me of that either,' he said with an air of alarm that made her chuckle. 'You teasing little shrew. What are you trying to do to me?'

'Cheer you up,' she said. 'You really need it.'

'Yes, I do. And I might have guessed you'd be the one to see it. Come on. Let's face them together.'

On the way down in the elevator he said, 'Mary's here. I saw her this afternoon.'

'And the children?'

'Briefly. None of us knew what to say, but that was because *he* was there.'

'He?'

'Ken, the guy who thinks he's going to replace me as their father. They're all in the same suite, a "family", Mary says.'

'How do they get on with Ken?'

'They seem to like him,' Darius sighed.

'Good.'

For a moment he scowled, but then sighed and said, 'All right, say it.'

'If they get on with their stepfather they'll be happier. And I know you won't spoil that because you love them too much.'

A faint ironic smile touched his lips. 'All right, teacher. I've taken the lesson on board.'

'Just make sure that you pay attention,' she commanded him severely.

His eyes swept over her glamorous appearance. 'I am paying attention,' he assured her. 'But that wasn't what you meant, was it?'

'No, it wasn't. Bad boy. Go to the back of the class.'

'Fine, I'll get an even better view of you from there.'

'Behave!'

'Aren't I allowed to say that you're beautiful and gorgeous and—?'

'No, you are *not* allowed to say it.'

'All right. I'll just think it.'

She'd done what she'd set out to do, put him in a cheerful mood for the evening. And nothing else mattered. She had to remember that!

As they emerged from the elevator downstairs they could see people already streaming towards the great room where the reception was to be held.

As soon as they entered Harriet saw their hosts on a slightly raised dais at the far end. There was Mary, smiling, greeting her guests. Beside her stood Ken, the man she was about to marry, and on the other side were the children, dressed up in formal clothes and looking uncomfortable.

Harriet was alive with curiosity to meet the woman Darius had loved and married, who had borne him two children, then preferred another man. An incredible decision, whispered the voice that she tried vainly to silence.

'Ready?' Darius murmured in her ear.

'Ready for anything.'

'Then forward into battle,'

She was aware of heads turned in curiosity as Mary's ex-husband advanced with another woman on his arm, and now she was glad he'd arrayed her in fine clothes so that she could do him proud.

Mary was a tall, elegant woman, with a beauty Harriet could only envy. But she also had a down-to-earth manner and an air of kindness that Harriet hadn't expected from the woman who'd spoken to her sharply on the phone.

'Mary, this is Harriet,' Darius said. 'Harriet, this is Mary, who was my wife until she decided she couldn't stand me any longer.'

There was real warmth in Mary's embrace, and her declaration, 'It's a pleasure to meet you.' But the way she then stood back and regarded Harriet was disconcerting. It was the look of someone who'd heard a lot and was intensely curious. It might have been Harriet's imagination that Mary then gave a little nod.

Ken, her fiancé, was quiet, conventional, pleasant-looking but unremarkable. He greeted Harriet in friendly fashion, acknowledged Darius and escaped as soon as possible.

'We've spoken on the telephone,' Mary said to Harriet. 'I recognise your voice.'

'Yes, Harriet was part of the lifeboat crew that saved me,' Darius said.

'Then she's my friend.' Suddenly Mary's eyes twinkled. 'And I was right about something else, wasn't I? You denied that you were his girlfriend but I knew.'

'Have a heart, Mary,' Darius growled.

'All right, I'll say no more. I don't want to embarrass either of you.'

But Darius was already uncomfortable, Harriet could tell. At the sight of his children his face lit up with relief and he opened his arms so that they could hug him.

She knew that Frankie was ten years old and Mark nine. Both were lively, attractive children with nice manners.

'Here she is, guys,' Darius said. 'This is the lifeboat lady that I told you about.'

Both of them stared.

'You work on a lifeboat?' Mark asked, awed.

'Not work. I'm on call if they need me.'

'But how often do you have to go out saving people?'

'It varies. Sometimes once a month, sometimes twice a day.'

'It must be ever so exciting,' Frankie breathed.

'Hey, she doesn't do it for fun,' Darius protested. 'I didn't find it exciting to be stuck in the water, wondering if I'd ever get out.'

'But Dad, she *saved* you,' Mark pointed out.

'Yes,' he agreed quietly. 'She saved me.'

He might have said more, but something he saw over their shoulders made him straighten up, tense.

'Hello, Father,' he said.

So that was Amos Falcon, Harriet thought. Research had made her familiar with his face, but the reality was startling. This was a fierce, uncompromising man with dark eyes shadowed by heavy brows. His mouth might once have been merely firm, but now it looked as though a lifetime of setting it in resolute lines had left it incapable of anything gentler. This was a giant, to be feared. And she did fear him, instinctively.

More troubling still was the astonishing resemblance between him and Darius. They were the same height and with broad shoulders, features that were similar, even handsome. They were undoubtedly father and son.

In how many ways? she wondered. Was Darius doomed to grow into a replica of a man everyone called awesome? Or was there still time for him to seek another path?

Darius drew her forward for introductions, and she was surprised to see that Amos studied her intently. Of course, he was naturally concerned to know about his son's companion. But she sensed there was more. His eyes, boring into her, seemed to combine knowledge, curiosity and harsh suspicion in equal measure. It was unnerving

He made a polite speech of gratitude for Darius's life, then introduced his wife, Janine, who smiled and also spoke of gratitude. She struck Harriet as a modest, retiring woman, which probably suited Amos.

'And this is my daughter, Freya,' she said, indicating a tall young woman beside her.

This was the wife the powerful Amos had chosen for Darius. She didn't look like the kind of female who would shrink back and let herself be a pawn. She was tall, fair, well, but not extravagantly dressed, with an air of self-possession. She shook Harriet's hand vigorously and said all the polite things before hailing Darius with an unmistakable air of sisterly derision. Harriet discovered that she liked Freya a lot.

There were more arrivals, people approaching the dais

to be greeted, and the crowd moved on and shifted her with it. When Darius began to lead her around the room, introducing her to people, she couldn't resist looking back and found Amos staring after her.

Glancing about her, Harriet was more than ever glad that she was dressed in style. This was a gathering of the rich and mighty, and at least she looked as though she belonged amongst them, however fake it might be.

It was clear that Darius really did belong in this gathering. Many of them knew him and spoke respectfully. They knew he'd taken a hit, but so had they, and his fortunes could yet recover, so they addressed him as they had always done, crossing their fingers.

Harriet found herself remembering the day she'd overheard him on the phone vowing, 'no mercy!' How long ago that seemed now that she'd discovered his other side. But these people had never discovered it, and wouldn't have believed it if she'd told them.

And nor, she realised, would Darius want them to believe it. Much of his power depended on a ruthless image.

'What's the matter?' he asked suddenly.

'Matter? Nothing?'

'Why are you giving me that curious look?'

'I didn't know I was.'

'What's going on in that mind of yours?'

'Nothing. My mind is a pure blank.'

He grinned. 'You're a very annoying woman, you know that?'

'Have you only just found that out?'

'I guess I'm still learning. Come on, let's have a good time.'

CHAPTER SEVEN

SUDDENLY Darius's face lit up at something he'd seen over Harriet's shoulder. '*Jackson, you young devil.* Where have you been?'

The young man approaching them was sufficiently like Darius to be his brother, yet better looking. His features were more regular, less interesting, she thought. Most women would have called him handsome.

He greeted Darius with a friendly thump on the shoulder and stood back to survey him with pleasure.

'I've been abroad,' he said. 'I just got back yesterday to find that nobody had seen hide nor hair of you for ages. Where did you vanish to?'

'Herringdean. I'm the unexpected owner of an island off the south coast. This lady—' he drew Harriet forward '—lives there and has been kind enough to be my guide and friend.'

Jackson beamed and engulfed her hand in his. 'I don't know how you put up with him,' he said.

'Neither do I,' she said, liking him immensely.

'Did I hear right? Herringdean? *The* Herringdean?'

'I don't know of any other,' she said.

Delight broke over his face. 'You've got fulmars there, haven't you?'

'Yes, plenty of them. They're beautiful.' Light dawned. 'Hey, I've seen you before, haven't I? On television?'

'I've done a programme or two,' he agreed. 'But never one about fulmars. Could you and I have a talk some time soon?'

'Of course we can.'

'Then you can really have a deep discussion about fulmars,' Darius observed. 'I don't know how you can bear the suspense.'

Laughing, the other two turned on him.

'They're birds,' Harriet said. 'Very big and lovely. They look like gulls but they're really petrels.'

'Fascinating!' said Darius, who wouldn't have known a gull from a petrel if they'd attacked him together.

'They nest high up on cliffs,' Harriet continued, 'and they're one of the beauties of Herringdean.'

Darius regarded her with comic irony. 'And I've owned these fabulous creatures all this time and you didn't tell me?'

'Nobody owns fulmars,' Harriet said. 'It's they who own the world, especially that bit of it called Herringdean.'

Jackson looked at her with appreciation. 'I see you're an expert,' he said. 'Don't waste yourself on this fellow. Let's go and have that talk now.'

'Yes, be off while I make some duty calls,' Darius said.

She was briefly afraid that the exchange might have offended him, but he kissed her cheek, saying, 'Take care of her, Jackson.'

Now she remembered Darius saying that his brother was a naturalist. 'Not an academic. He just works a lot with animals and charities. Does TV a bit, goes off on expeditions. You'd find him interesting.'

And she did. Jackson knew his stuff, and as she also

knew hers they plunged into a knowledgeable discussion that pleased them both.

Darius did his duty, going from acquaintance to acquaintance, saying the right things, avoiding the wrong things, smiling mechanically, performing as expected. Nothing in his demeanour revealed that he was intensely conscious of Harriet and Jackson sitting at a side table, their heads close together, each so absorbed that they seemed to have forgotten the rest of the world.

Gradually, he managed to get near enough to eavesdrop but what he heard brought him no comfort. He couldn't discern every word, but Jackson clearly said, 'It depends whether you're talking about northern fulmars or southern fulmars…'

His last words were drowned out, but then Harriet said, 'It's a pity that…any old rubbish…almost makes you want to…'

Jackson asked a question and she replied eagerly, 'That's always the way with *Procellariidae*, don't you think?'

'*What?*'

Jackson looked up and grinned. 'Here's my brother. Perhaps you'd better return to him before he goes out of his mind.'

He touched Darius on the shoulder and departed. Darius drew Harriet's arm through his, saying, 'I hardly dare ask what you were talking about. What the blue blazes are procellar—whatever?'

'*Procellariidae*. It's just the name of the family that fulmars belong to, just like crows and magpies are *Corvids*—'

'Are they really? You'll be telling me next that wrens are dinosaurs.'

'Oh, no, wrens are *Troglodytidae*.' Her lips twitched.

'There, and you thought of me as a silly little creature who didn't know any long words.'

'Well, if I was foolish enough to think that you've made me sorry. I feel as if I've been walked over by hobnailed boots.'

'Good,' she teased. 'Serve you right.'

She was looking up at him with gleaming eyes, and he couldn't have stopped himself responding, however much he wanted to. But he didn't want to. He wanted to take her hand and follow her into the world where only she could take him—the world of laughter and good fellowship that had been closed to him before but now seemed to open invitingly whenever she was there.

A few yards away Jackson watched them, unnoticed, a curious expression on his face. After a while he smiled as though he'd seen something that satisfied him.

Harriet had tried to prepare herself to cope among Darius's family. She told herself that she was ready for Mary, for Freya, even for Amos. But it was the children who surprised her. After doing their social duty, Frankie and Mark effectively took her prisoner, corralling her into a corner and sitting one each side, lest she have ideas of escape. Like all the best hostage-takers, they provided her with excellent food and drink, but there was no doubt they meant business.

First she had to tell the story of Darius's rescue, suitably edited for their childish ears. Then they wanted to hear about other rescue trips, listening in awed silence, until Mark said breathlessly, 'But aren't you scared?'

She thought for a moment. 'Not really.'

'Not even when it's terribly dangerous?' Frankie persisted.

'There isn't time to be scared. There's always so much to do.'

Frankie looked around before leaning forward and whispering, 'It's more fun when it's dangerous, isn't it?'

Harriet hesitated, aware of a yawning pit at her feet. She must be careful what she said to children. Especially these two. Frankie's gleaming eyes showed that she already had her own opinion of the joys of danger.

'No,' Harriet said, trying to sound firm. 'And that is a very irresponsible point of view. Danger has to be taken seriously.'

'Yes, Mrs Connor,' Frankie said, straight-faced.

'Harry. My friends call me Harry, like yours call you Frankie.'

United by the bond, they shook hands.

She liked them both enormously, but with Frankie she also had the connection of like recognising like. As a child, she too had felt that danger could be fun. Truth to tell, she still often found it so, as long as it was only her own. Other people's peril had to be taken seriously, but there was a 'ping' about fighting for one's own survival that most people wouldn't understand, and certainly not sympathise with.

Her father had lectured her about being sensible. Now she had passed on the lecture to the next generation, just as she would have done with a child of her own, she thought wistfully.

But she had no children and probably never would have. Darius's offspring would have to be her consolation.

'Go on about Herringdean,' Mark begged. 'Why did you join the lifeboats?'

'I followed my father. He taught me to love being on the water. I've got a little yacht that I sail whenever I can. Every year Herringdean has a regatta, and I compete in a lot of the races. I win some too.' She added proudly, 'I've got all sorts of trophies.'

'Tell, tell,' they demanded.

They were as sailing-crazy as she was herself but, living in London, had fewer chances to indulge their passion.

'Mum takes us on holiday to the seaside,' Frankie said, 'and she gets someone to take us out in a boat, but then we have to come home.'

'What about your father?' Harriet asked. 'Does he go out in the boat with you?'

'He's never been there,' Frankie said. 'He was always too busy to come on holiday.'

'That's very sad,' Harriet said, meaning it. 'He misses so much.'

'He nearly came once,' Mark recalled. 'We were going to have a wonderful time together, but at the last minute he got a call and said he had to stay at home. I overheard him on the phone—he was trying to stop some deal from falling apart. He said he'd join us as soon as he could, but he never did. It was soon after that he and Mum split up. Now we don't go at all.'

Frankie took a deep breath. 'Harry, do you think—?'

'Ah, there you are, you two,' came Mary's voice from nearby. 'I've got someone for you to meet.'

They groaned but got up obediently. Harriet felt a pang of dismay, wondering if Mary had deliberately sought to separate her from the children. And had she heard Frankie call her Harry? If so, was she resentful at their instant bond?

But the smile Mary gave her before hurrying away was unreadable.

Socially, she knew she was a success. Janine and Freya spoke to her pleasantly, Marcel and Jackson claimed her company, while Amos looked on. When he did address her, his manner was courteous but distant, as though he was reserving judgement.

None of the other men there reserved judgement. Admiring glances followed her everywhere and when the dancing started she had her pick of partners. Jackson was at the head of the queue, finally yielding to Marcel.

'Whatever is Darius thinking of to leave you alone?' Marcel asked as they hot-footed it around the floor.

'Darius has urgent things to attend to,' she said primly. 'I don't get in his way.'

'*Sacre bleu!* You talk like that?' he demanded, aghast.

'Sometimes I do,' she said mischievously. 'Sometimes I don't.'

'You keep him guessing?'

'Definitely.'

'So you believe in ill-treating him?'

'It has its uses.'

'Well, then, you must do this. In the end he will rebel, the two of you will quarrel, and it will be my turn.'

Harriet couldn't have said what made her choose her next words. She'd never been a flirt or a tease, but a delightfully wicked impulse made her say, 'Oh, you're going to wait your turn?'

'If I have to. Does brother Darius know you tease other men?'

'Darius knows exactly what I want him to know.'

'I see. I must remember that. I wonder what he did to be such a lucky man.'

She seemed to consider. 'I think he's still wondering that too. Some day I'll tell him.'

That made him roar with laughter. She joined in, relishing the experience of flirting on the edge of indiscretion, a pleasure she'd never known before. Suddenly the world was full of new delights, and she felt herself becoming slightly dizzy.

No doubt it was coincidence that made Darius appear

at that moment. Marcel made a resigned face and yielded, kissing her hand before he departed.

'Until the next time,' he said.

'Do I get a little of your company at last?' Darius asked. 'I seem to be the only person you're not spending time with.'

'Just trying to do you credit,' she said. 'You wouldn't want to be known as the man who accompanied a little brown mouse, would you?'

'I don't think there's much fear of that,' he said. 'I'm beginning to think I've never really known you.'

'Is that so surprising?' she asked. 'We met only a few weeks ago. Neither of us really knows anything about the other.'

'No, we don't,' he said slowly. 'You've taken me by surprise so many times… You'd think I'd realise by now…'

'Maybe we never realise,' she whispered.

The evening was drawing to a close. The bride- and groom-to-be embraced each other for the last waltz, and other dancers joined in. Darius took her hand and held it gently for a moment.

'My turn,' he said. 'Unless you object.'

'No,' she murmured. 'I don't object.'

No words could express how much she didn't object to dancing with Darius as he took her into his arms. Suddenly the most vibrant sensation she'd ever known was the light touch of his hand on her back, drawing her close but not as close as she would have liked. His hand holding hers seemed to whisper of that other time when he'd clung to her in a gesture that had transformed the world.

And then it had been transformed again, and yet again, with how many more to come? Once she would have wished she knew the answer to that, but now she was content to let the path lead where it might, as long as it ultimately led to him. In the enchanted atmosphere of tonight that didn't seem as crazily impossible as it normally would.

There was warm affection in his smile, but was it real or only part of tonight's performance? Or could she make it real? Was Cinderella's power great enough for that?

The music was coming to an end. The ball was over.

But there would be another ball tomorrow, and Prince Charming might yet fit the glass slipper on her foot.

Darius? she thought. Prince Charming?

Well, it took all sorts.

'Is everything all right?' he asked, searching her face.

'Yes,' she said contentedly. 'Everything's all right.'

As they went upstairs he said, 'You were wonderful. Everything I hoped.'

'I floundered a bit.'

'No, you didn't. My kids love you, even Mary thinks you're terrific. You're a star.'

'So I really have helped you?' she asked hopefully.

'More than you'll ever know. And tomorrow's going to be even better.'

'Would you like to come in and talk about it?' Harriet ventured to suggest. 'You can give me my instructions for tomorrow.'

For a moment she thought he would agree, but then a wry look came over his face.

'I'd love to but…things to do. You know how it is.'

'Yes,' she said a touch sadly, 'I know how it is.'

'And besides, you don't need any instructions from me. You've got it all sussed. Now, go and have a good sleep.'

She smiled up at him. 'Goodnight.'

He didn't reply at first, just stood looking down at her with an expression more gentle than she had ever seen before and the faintest smile on his lips. But then the smile faded, became tight and constrained.

'Goodnight,' he said, and moved away.

For a moment Harriet was too dazed to know where she was or what was happening to her. Hearing her door close, she realised that she had entered her room without even being aware of it. As if from a great distance, she heard his own door being closed.

He'd been about to kiss her. She knew it beyond a shadow of doubt. It had been there in his face, until he changed his mind, probably remembering that other time on the beach when she'd told him to back off. How could she have known then that by now she would feel so differently?

So much had changed tonight. She'd been practically the belle of the ball, surrounded by admirers, seeing herself through their eyes but trapped inside her ivory tower. But it was she who, only yesterday, had slammed shut the door of that tower, and she could blame nobody but herself.

Not so much Cinderella as the Sleeping Beauty.

'Except that nobody could consider me a beauty,' she mused wryly.

But Darius had thought so, perhaps only for a brief moment but a little feminine strategy might have transformed that moment into long-lasting joy. Had retreating into the tower, protecting her safety at the expense of life's joy, really been the right thing to do?

'Curses!' she muttered. 'Why did this have to happen now?'

Brooding thus, she snuggled down in the huge bed, wishing it was smaller. Its size seemed to demand two people and she was attacked by a feeling of loneliness.

It was still dark when she awoke. The illuminated clock showed that three hours had passed since they had parted and she had the feeling that something strange was happening. After a moment she realised that a phone was ringing.

It seemed to come from the other side of the wall, so surely Darius would answer it soon. But it went on and on. Nobody was going to answer it.

Perhaps the sound came from somewhere else? She slipped out of bed, threw on her wrap and went out into the dark corridor. Now there was no doubt. It was Darius's phone and there was nobody to answer it.

He wasn't there. He was spending the night with someone else. And she was a fool not to have realised that it was bound to happen. In London there would be a hundred women he could turn to. Returning to her own room, she had to stop herself slamming the door. She had no right to feel insulted or neglected, but that didn't help.

So, who? Freya? Perhaps he really needed his father's money that much. Or one of the numerous females who'd made eyes at him that evening?

She threw herself back down onto the bed but sleep was impossible, and now she wondered how she could get through tomorrow. How could she look at him without an accusation in her eyes, however illogical?

Restlessly, she jumped up and began to pace the room. From the street outside came the sound of a car and she drew aside the curtain to look down.

Then she grew still as she saw the passenger get out. It was Darius, and he was weighed down with baggage. Three large suitcases were offloaded onto the pavement and collected by the porter, then they disappeared into the hotel.

Harriet scurried to her door, listening. She heard the elevator arrive, the doors open and the sound of a trolley being wheeled across the floor, stopping outside the room next to hers. Only then did she look out.

Darius was opening his door, indicating for the porter to

take the luggage in. When the man had departed he seemed to notice Harriet.

'Sorry if the racket disturbed you.'

'It didn't. I happened to see you arrive downstairs. You look worn out.'

'I've been to my apartment to collect a few things. At least, it was meant to be a few things, but once I started I couldn't stop.'

'You mean—that's where you've been all this time?' she breathed.

'Yes, I decided I couldn't be in London without going home for a few hours. I've had someone going in to collect any mail that arrived, but there was still plenty of stuff on the mat. I didn't mean to stay so long but things built up. What's the matter? What's funny?'

'Nothing,' she said in a trembling voice.

'Then why are you laughing?'

'I'm not—not really.'

'Yes, you are. What's so funny at this hour?'

'You wouldn't understand. Go to bed quickly. I'll see you in the morning.'

She escaped before she could give herself away any more. It was vital to be alone to throw herself on her bed, to laugh and cry, and marvel at where the path was leading her.

Now for the big one.

That was her thought as she sat before the mirror next morning, watching as her make-up was again applied by an expert.

Today her clothes were less ostentatiously glamorous, although no less costly, a matching dress and jacket in light grey heavy silk. Around her neck she wore the diamond pendant.

Now the attendants had gone and there was just time for one last important job. Quickly, she dialled her neighbour's number.

'Hi, Jenny, is everything all right?—Lovely—he's not off his food, is he?— Oh, good, they're his favourite bones but I was afraid he might pine—oh, please fetch him.'

Marcel and Jackson, knocking on their brother's door, found it opened promptly.

'I'm honoured,' he said ironically.

'Not you, her,' Jackson informed him. 'Do you think we're going to miss the chance to be seen with the most gorgeous girl since—? Is this her door? Good.'

All three of them raised their hands, but before they could knock they heard Harriet's voice inside.

'Oh, darling, do you miss me? I miss you so much. I'll be home soon. I love you more than anyone in the world.'

Jackson and Marcel stared at their brother.

'A *ménage à trois*?' Marcel demanded, aghast. 'You?'

'Not in a million years,' Darius declared. 'I leave those kind of shenanigans to you.'

'But she was talking to the one she loves *more than anyone in the world.*'

'She was talking to her dog,' Darius said, grinning. 'She does that a lot. She left him with a friend and she called him as soon as we arrived.'

Jackson nodded. 'She's probably had him since she was a child.'

'No, he belonged to her husband who died a year ago.'

'Ah!' Enlightenment settled over Marcel. 'Then perhaps it is the dead husband whom she loves more than—'

'Shall we be going?' Darius interrupted him, knocking. 'Harriet, are you ready in there?'

'Coming!' She opened the door and stood basking in their looks of admiration.

Instantly, Marcel and Jackson extended their hands to her, but Darius stayed firm.

'Back off, you two,' he said, drawing her hand into the crook of his elbow. 'She's mine.'

And Harriet thought she detected a note of pride in his voice, if only she could allow herself to believe it.

Heads held high, they went downstairs to where the ceremony would take place. It would be a civil ceremony, but the venue had been done up to emulate the grandeur of a church. There were flowers everywhere and chairs laid out in rows, while at the far end a choir was assembling.

It was almost time to begin. Ken took his place and stood waiting, his eyes fixed on the door through which his bride would come.

At last Mary appeared and began to walk slowly towards him. She was magnificently dressed in a long gown of saffron coloured satin, a diamond tiara on her head. Behind her walked Frankie and Mark.

What would Darius be feeling now, she wondered, as his one-time beloved married another man and his children became part of another family? He was between her and the procession, so that his face was turned away, and she could only wonder about his expression. But she guessed it would reveal nothing.

As the children passed she saw that Frankie wore a frilly bridesmaid dress and Mark had a page's costume, also frilly. How he would hate that, she thought.

As if to confirm it, he glanced up at her and made a face of helpless resignation. She made a face back, conveying sympathy. By chance, Darius happened to turn his head in time to see them both.

'Poor Mark,' she murmured.

The procession was slowing down, bringing Mark to a brief halt. Just a couple of seconds but it was enough for

Darius to put his hand on his son's shoulder and grunt, 'Don't give up, lad.'

Then they were on their way again, with only the memory of Mark's look of amazed gratitude at his father.

Slowly, the ceremony advanced until the moment when the bride took her groom's hand, looking up into his face and saying fervently, 'You are mine, and I am yours. We will be together for always, and no other man will ever live in my heart.'

Conventional words for a wedding, but how did they sound to the man who had once been her husband? Carefully, Harriet turned her head, hoping to catch a sideways glimpse of his face, only to find it turned towards her. He wasn't looking at the couple swearing their love. His gaze was fixed on her, and something in it made her turn quickly away.

A few feet away, Amos and his family were seated, their chairs at an angle that enabled Amos to see Darius and Harriet clearly. His eyes narrowed, an expression that Jackson recognised with a sigh and that made him exchange a glance with Marcel.

They knew that look on their father's face, and it didn't bode well.

CHAPTER EIGHT

AS THEY walked out afterwards Amos fell into step beside Jackson, speaking in a low voice. 'What do you know about her?'

'Only that she's delightful, and a very good influence on Darius.'

'And just what does that mean?'

'I've been watching them together.' Jackson fell silent.

'And?' Amos demanded. *'And?'*

'He was laughing.'

'What are you talking about?'

'It's true. Darius was laughing.'

'I've seen that too,' Marcel put in. 'And you know what makes him laugh? She makes fun of him.'

'She makes fun of him? And he likes it? Rubbish.'

'They share jokes,' Jackson agreed. 'I've seen them and heard some of the things they say. Daft remarks tossed back and forth, things that wouldn't make any sense to other people, but they understand each other, and they laugh together. I've never seen that in Darius before. She's transformed him.'

Amos didn't answer this, but he strode on ahead and waited for Darius to appear. He nodded briefly at Harriet and jerked his head for his son to follow him.

'What is it, Father?' Darius asked.

'We need to talk.'

'Right now? They're just starting the reception.'

'It won't take long.'

He walked away without stopping until they'd both entered a little side room and closed the door. Then Amos turned on him.

'I gather things are getting worse.'

Darius hesitated a moment before saying, 'Financially, they're not going well but in other ways—'

Amos brushed this disclaimer aside. 'I was speaking financially.'

'Of course,' Darius murmured.

'You can't raise the loans you need, and when you put property up for sale it won't raise the asking price.'

'May I ask how you know these details?' Darius said grimly.

'You don't imagine there are any secrets, do you?'

'Not from you.'

'You ought to be here in London, working things out. Instead, you waste time on that island that can hardly be worth—well, what *is* it worth?'

'You mean in money terms?' Darius asked in a strange voice.

'Don't play games with me. Of course I mean money. How much could you raise from it?'

'I have no idea.'

'But you've been living there for weeks; you must have investigated.'

'In a sort of way,' he said carefully. 'But it's too soon to form conclusions. I don't want to rush things.'

'I suppose that's the influence of the young woman you brought with you. I hope you're not taking her too seriously.'

'As seriously as a man takes a woman who saved his life.'

'Don't make too much of that. It means nothing to her. It's just her job.'

'But it's not,' Darius said fiercely. 'She isn't employed by the Lifeboat Institution, she's a volunteer. She has an ordinary job, but night and day she's ready to drop everything for the people who need her, even if their cries for help come at awkward moments. She doesn't think of herself, she thinks of them.'

'All right, all right, spare me the speech,' Amos said in a bored voice. 'I get the point. Naturally, I expressed my gratitude and of course you've shown your own gratitude by bringing her here. I hope she enjoys herself. But let it end there. She's no real use to you. She doesn't have a penny and she won't understand your way of life.'

'And how do you know what she has and hasn't?' Darius demanded harshly. 'Have you been having her watched, because if you've dared—'

'No need to be melodramatic. I've merely made a few enquiries. She seems a decent sort, lives a quiet life.'

'As you'd expect from a widow grieving for the husband she loved, and who loved her.'

Amos's smile was coldly self-satisfied. 'Ah, so you don't know. I wondered.'

'Know about what? What the hell are you talking about?'

'Did she ever take you to see her husband's grave?'

'Of course not. Naturally, she prefers to keep it private.'

'Have you known her visit that grave at all?'

'How could I know?'

'How could you indeed since she takes such care to hide the truth? But you'll find the answer here.' He thrust a sheet of paper in Darius's hand. 'Read it and find out just how cunningly she's been keeping her secrets. Then see how much of a heroine she looks.'

Darius took the paper and read its contents. Then he grew very still, trying to control his mounting outrage.

His eyes were hard as he looked up at his father, then down again at the paper in his hand. 'Los Angeles,' he murmured.

'Brad Connor died in a car crash in Los Angeles, and he's buried out there,' Amos said.

'And you read something into that? He was in the tourist industry, so he probably travelled a lot.'

'He wasn't there to work; he was living with the woman he planned to marry as soon as his divorce came through.'

'You can't know that,' Darius declared. But he knew as he spoke that Amos could find out anything he liked. It had always been one of the things that inspired admiration for his business abilities, but now Darius could feel only a horror that he'd never known before.

'Of course I know,' Amos snapped. 'I know everything that's been happening to you on that island.'

'You've dared to plant spies?'

'I've taken steps to assess the situation. That's always been my way and you know it. You should be grateful. Do you think I'd stand back and see you run into danger without doing anything?'

'I'm not in any danger.'

'You're in danger of becoming sentimental, and that's one thing you can't afford. I'd hoped by now you'd be seeing things more sensibly but, since you're not, let me spell it out. This young woman has deceived you, presenting a picture of her life that's far from the truth.'

'She has not deceived me,' Darius snapped. 'She's kept

things to herself, but why shouldn't she? Her personal trag-edy is none of my business. If she can't bear to talk about it, that's up to her.'

His eyes were full of fury and for the first time it dawned on Amos that he'd miscalculated. His son was every bit as enraged as he'd wanted him to be, but his anger was di-rected not against Harriet, but against the man who sought to damage her. Amos decided that it was time to change tack. Reasoning might work better.

'I understand that,' he said, 'but it doesn't change the fact that she's holding things back while pretending to be open. You don't know her as well as you thought you did. What other secrets is she concealing?'

'Whatever they are, she'll confide in me in her own good time, *if she wants to*.'

'Just stop and think what's going on in her head. One husband let her down, so next time she's going to make certain that she scores. She's out to marry you with her eyes on the divorce settlement she'll eventually claim.'

Darius gave a harsh laugh. 'Out to marry me? You know nothing. She's here as my companion, no more. I had to promise to stick to her rules or she wouldn't have come.'

Amos groaned and abandoned reasoning as useless. 'How can any son of mine be so naïve? That's the oldest trick in the book.'

'She doesn't go in for tricks,' Darius said. 'She's as honest as the day is long. You have no idea.'

'You've really got it bad, haven't you?' Amos said in a voice that verged on contempt.

'If you mean that I'm in love with her, you're wrong. Harriet and I are friends. With her I've found a kind of friendship I didn't know existed. I can talk to her with-out wondering if she'll make use of the information. She gives far more than she takes, and that's something I never thought to find in anyone. Try to understand. She's a revelation. I didn't know women like her existed, and I'm not going to do anything to spoil it.'

Amos regarded him with pity. 'A revelation—unlike any other woman,' he echoed. 'Well, I'll say this for her. She's more skilled and astute than I gave her credit for. All right, maybe she's not out to marry you. Perhaps she's just stringing you along for the sake of her island friends. After all, you're the power there. It would pay her to get on your right side.'

'Stop it!' Darius raged. 'If you know what's good for you, stop it *now*!'

'Or what? Is my son threatening me? I really did underestimate her, didn't I? All right, we'll say no more. I tried to warn you but there's no helping a fool.'

'Maybe I am a fool,' Darius said. 'And maybe I'm happy to settle for that.'

'That makes you an even bigger fool.'

'If you dare make yourself unpleasant to Harriet—'

'I've no intention of doing so. Now, it's time we were getting back to the party.'

He strode out. As he walked through the door Darius saw him position a smile on his face, so that he appeared to the assembled company wearing the proper mask.

Suddenly Darius felt sick.

It was an effort to get his own mask in place and he knew he was less successful than his father, managing only an air of calm that covered the turmoil within. Harriet was sitting with her arm across the empty seat beside her, looking around worriedly. Someone spoke to her and she answered briefly before returning to her troubled search. It was as though the world had stopped in its tracks until she found what she was looking for.

Then she saw Darius and he drew in his breath at the

transformation. Suddenly it was as though she was illuminated from inside, radiant, joyful.

'I'm sorry,' he said, going to sit beside her. 'I got waylaid. Forgive my bad manners.'

'Is everything all right?'

'Everything's fine.' He laid his hand over hers. 'Nothing for you to worry about.'

A waiter poured champagne for them both.

'Now, let's forget everything else and enjoy ourselves,' Darius said, raising his glass to clink hers.

Around the various tables, his family observed them. His brothers grinned. His stepsister smiled with relief. His children rubbed their hands. His father scowled.

It was time for the speeches. The best man spoke, the bride and groom talked eloquently. Various other guests proposed toasts. Darius was barely aware of it. He was conscious only of Harriet beside him, wondering if she was remembering the joy of her own wedding, and the marriage that had ended in tragedy. But he could detect nothing in her manner that gave him a clue. Her barriers were in place.

He'd meant it when he'd told his father that he didn't feel deceived that she had kept her secrets. It was yet more proof of their special friendship that he made no claims on her, demanded no rights.

But he knew a faint sadness that she hadn't felt able to confide in him.

Your fault, he told himself. *If you'd shut up talking about yourself for five minutes she might get a word in edgeways.*

That eased his mind briefly, but he could remember a couple of times when the talk had strayed to her husband and she'd diverted it to something else. The truth was she didn't want to open up to him. That was her right. He'd said so and he believed it. But it hurt.

Nor could he entirely escape the suspicion that if she hadn't warned him off he would have sought more than friendship. She was beautiful, not conventionally, like other women, but with a mysterious enchantment that came from within and that beckoned him on.

He'd made promises about keeping his distance but, with a woman like this, how could a real man keep such insane promises?

Now waiters were clearing away for the dancing. The bridal couple took the floor and were soon joined by the rest of the crowd.

'This time I'm seizing you first,' Darius said firmly. 'Before I get trampled in the rush.'

'Nonsense,' she said tenderly.

'It isn't nonsense. Of course it's nice when the lady on your arm turns out to be the belle of the ball, but it has its troublesome moments too. I don't like sharing.'

'Neither do I, but we both have to do our social duty.'

'Ah, I see. You've gone into teasing mode.'

'Why not? I enjoy new experiences and, after all, you brought me here to help stage a performance. Think of me as a piece of stage scenery. Under this dress I'm just wood and plaster. Hey, what are you doing?'

'Just checking the stage scenery,' he said, letting his hand drift around her waist until it sank immodestly over her hips. 'It doesn't feel like any wood and plaster I've ever known.'

It was shocking and she knew she should tell him to move his hand from where it lay over the smooth grey silk, softly caressing the movements against his fingers. But a little pulse was beating in her throat and she couldn't get the words out. And probably nobody could see it in the crowd, she reassured herself.

She was suffused by a warmth and sweetness so intense that it made her dizzy. She wanted to dance like this for ever, his arms around her, his body close to hers, and never have to think of anything else again.

The music was slowing, couples were pulling apart. Marcel presented himself expectantly.

'Go to blazes,' Darius told him pleasantly.

'Certainly,' Marcel said, and vanished.

Harriet was barely aware of Marcel, or any of their surroundings. Lost in a dream, she let herself drift into a new world, refusing to heed the warnings of danger, although she knew that danger would intrude in the end. But let it, she thought. First she would have her moment, and cherish its memory to see her through the dark times.

With a sigh, she felt his movements slow as this dance too came to an end, and she knew that he would not claim her again. The moment had come and gone until, perhaps, another time.

Harriet wondered if it could possibly have been the same for him, but when she looked into his face she saw that it was troubled.

'What's on your mind?' she asked. 'Something's worrying you. I know it. Tell me.'

For a moment he hesitated on the verge of telling her about his father and what he'd learned, but then he backed off, unable to risk hurting her.

'Can't you tell your friend what's wrong?' she asked gently.

Once, younger and more careless, he'd joked that at all costs a man should avoid a woman who understood him too well. How often had he avoided Mary's piercing mental gaze! Yet with this woman he only felt a renewed sense of comfort, as though her hand had once again stretched out to offer safety.

'No,' he said softly. 'Nothing is wrong.' And at that moment he meant it.

It was just like his brothers to barge in, he thought, finally yielding to Marcel. But there was always later. Patience would bring him everything.

After that they both concentrated on their social duty. Harriet was never short of partners, until finally she glanced up to find Amos approaching, the very picture of geniality.

'I've been hoping to dance with you but there were so many men ahead of me.' He held out his hand. 'Please say I'm not too late.'

'Of course not,' she said, smiling and taking his hand.

Heads turned as he led her onto the floor, the crowd parted for them, and there was a smattering of applause as he drew her into the dance. Darius, passing the time with Freya, turned his head casually, then grew tense.

'What the devil—?' he breathed.

'He seems quite charmed with Harriet,' Freya said. 'Look at the way he's smiling, practically welcoming her into the family.' She gave Darius an amused look. 'I should be grateful to her, really. It helps take the pressure off me, *brother, dear.*'

'Look at them,' he said distractedly. 'Why is he laughing like that?'

'She's laughing too,' Freya pointed out. 'Obviously they're getting on well. He can be so grim, it's nice to see him putting himself out to be nice to her.'

But for Darius, who knew what really lay behind Amos's 'charm', every moment was torment. He was trying to lure Harriet into a trap, hoping she would say something he could use against her. Darius had often seen him wear a pleasant mask as long as it could be useful, and had thought little of it.

But this was different. This was Harriet—great-hearted, innocent, vulnerable—and he was filled with desire to protect her at all costs.

'Dance with me,' he said, taking Freya's hand.

She was too astute to mistake his motive, especially when she realised how determinedly he steered her in the direction of the other couple.

'Is this near enough for you?' she asked.

'Only just. Can you hear what he's saying?'

'Something about a shop on Herringdean—an antique shop—since when was he interested in antiques?'

'Since he found out she owned one,' Darius growled.

'Now he's talking money—how much is the shop worth?'

'Damn him!'

'Don't act surprised. That's always his first thought. Hey, he's watching us. Let's teach him a lesson.'

'How?'

'Look deep into my eyes, then he'll think what a good son you're being. You never know, he might solve all your problems with one cheque.'

'Yes, but he'd post-date it so that I'd have to marry you first.'

'Never fear. I'll avoid that catastrophe with my last breath.'

'So will I,' he assured her cheerfully.

They finished the dance with no hard feelings on either side.

When Amos had bid her farewell and departed, Harriet went to quench her thirst with an orange juice. Standing beside a large potted plant, she was only vaguely aware of movement from the other side until she heard Mary's voice say, 'Wherever did you find that marvellous girl?'

And Darius's eager reply. 'Harriet is marvellous, isn't she? I'm glad you like her.'

'Are you surprised? Did you think I'd be jealous? On the contrary, she's doing me a great favour. If you've got her, I don't have to feel guilty about leaving you. And the children like her, so I can send them to stay with you with an easy mind.'

'Do you really mean that?' Darius demanded urgently.

'I know you thought I was trying to separate you from them, but I wasn't. It's just that you hurt them so often with your stupidity.'

'There was a lot I didn't understand, but now—'

'But now things are beginning to change, and they'll go on changing as long as you stick with her. She's good for you, Darius. You've become almost human.'

'I never thought to hear you say that, Mary.'

'I never thought to be able to say it. That's why Mark and Frankie will be going to my mother while Ken and I are on honeymoon. They'd much rather have come to you in Herringdean, but I honestly didn't think you'd cope on your own. Now it's different.'

'Too late to send them to me?'

'My mother is so looking forward to having them. I can't disappoint her now. But there's plenty of time in the future. Keep up the good work. The kids are really happy about Harriet.'

'I know, and I can't tell you how much that means to me.'

'Well, make sure you keep her for good. You're a clever man and, believe me, that's the clever thing to do.'

They moved away, leaving Harriet deep in thought.

The evening was drawing to a close. Bride and groom

withdrew and reappeared in outdoor clothes. Cars were at the door. Mark and Frankie said their farewells to Darius and Harriet before being scooped up by their grandmother and swept off to her home on the other side of London.

'Are you tired?' Darius asked Harriet, who was yawning.

'Mmm, a bit sleepy. You did say we're going early tomorrow, didn't you?'

'That's right. Time for bed.'

On the way up in the elevator he slipped his arm around her. 'Did you enjoy it?'

'Oh, yes, it was lovely. Everyone was so nice to me, especially your father.'

'Yes, I saw the two of you dancing.'

'I couldn't believe it when he asked me, but he was terribly gallant and charming.'

'You should beware my father's charm,' Darius said wryly.

'Oh, I know he was just being polite but…I don't know… he was nice. He asked me about my antique shop, said he understood antiques were very profitable these days. I had to admit that it's as much of a souvenir shop for tourists as an antique shop. He laughed and said that was life and nothing was really the way it seemed, was it? Hey, careful. Don't squash me.'

'Sorry,' he said, relaxing the arm that he'd tightened sharply about her. Listening to her innocent pleasure when he knew how misguided it was brought a return of the rage that had attacked him earlier. But now it was a million times more intense, nearly blinding him with the desire to lash out against her enemy.

From the start he'd known of her strength, her defiance, her ability to cope, essential in a lifesaver. Suddenly he was discovering her other side, the one that could be slightly naïve, that believed the best of people, the side she hid behind cheerful masks.

But the face she turned up to him now wore no mask. It was defenceless, the mouth soft, the eyes wide and trusting. He knew it would be a sin to betray that trust by kissing her, no matter how much he longed to. So he contented himself with brushing her cheek with his fingertips, and felt her relax against him.

What he might have done next he never knew, for the elevator reached their floor, the doors opened and the world rushed in on them again.

Now she was smiling brightly in a way that set him once more at a distance.

'Sleep tight,' he told her at her door. 'We have to be up with the dawn.'

'I'll be there,' she promised. 'Goodnight.'

He thought she would give him a final look so that the sweet connection they had established might live again. But he was facing a closed door.

Inside her room, Harriet stood in darkness, listening as his footsteps moved away to his own door.

Her heart was heavy. Midnight had struck and Cinders had been forced to leave, not running away and leaving a shoe, but escorted by the Prince who'd been tempted only briefly before his common sense had rescued him.

It's over. All over. Finished. Done with. Get undressed, go to bed, and stop indulging in fantasies. Didn't you learn anything from last time?

Switching on the bedside lamp, she stripped off her beautiful attire with ruthless fingers and replaced it with plain cotton pyjamas. Her packing was done at top speed, and then she was ready for bed. Defiantly, she got under the duvet and switched out the light.

There was a knock at the door.
'Who is it?' she asked without opening.
'It's me.'

CHAPTER NINE

HARRIET opened the door a crack and saw him. He'd removed his jacket and bow tie and his shirt was torn open at the throat.

'Can I talk to you?'

She stood back as he went past her. She would have turned on the bedside lamp but he stayed her hand.

'Better just let me talk. I owe you an apology for my behaviour tonight.'

'Do you? You didn't offend me.'

'That's very sweet of you, but I got a bit possessive in a way that I promised not to. Just friends we said but I didn't really stick to that, did I? I hadn't expected you to look so beautiful—'

'Thanks,' she said wryly.

'No, I didn't mean that,' he said hastily. 'Oh, heavens, I'm making a mess of this. I only wanted to say that you were a hundred times more wonderful than I'd dared to hope and...*Harriet!*'

Then his arms were around her, pulling her tightly against him, and all the sensible restraint drained out of her as she received the kiss she'd been longing for, never completely admitting her own desire. Now there was no chance of denying it to herself or him. She felt herself soften and fall against him, reaching out so that he was enfolded in her arms as she was enfolded in his.

Her hands were exploring him, the fingers weaving into his hair before drifting down to his face. He raised his head from hers, looking down with a question in his eyes, as though wondering if he only imagined her passionate response.

'Harriet,' he whispered, 'why have we…?'

'Shh!' She silenced him with her fingertips over his mouth. 'Don't speak. Words are dangerous. They mean nothing.'

She was right, he realised with a sense of relief. Words were nothing when he had her body against his. He could feel the cheap cotton against his hands and wondered how any woman could feel so lusciously desirable in those almost masculine pyjamas. They taunted him, hiding her beautiful body while suggesting just enough of it to strain his self-control.

Harriet felt as though she had lived this moment before, earlier that evening when he'd allowed his hand to drift indiscreetly behind her dress, but then been forced by propriety to restrain himself. She hadn't wanted restraint either in him or herself, but she'd had no choice.

But she had choice now. She could choose to be warm, intimate, seductive, enticing, passionate. Anything but restrained. Her breathing came fast as he kissed her again and again, little swift kisses covering her face, her forehead, her nose, her eyes, mouth, then sliding lower to her neck.

He was so skilled, she thought in delirious delight. They might have been one person, so sensitively did he know the right way to rouse her—to make her want him—want him more—

'Make sure you keep her for good…'

Without warning, the words screamed at her. Frantically, she fought them off but they danced in her consciousness.

'You're a clever man...'

She'd known that but never thought what it meant—until now—

'Keep her for good...the clever thing to do...the clever thing to do...'

'Kiss me,' he whispered. 'Kiss me as I kiss you... please...'

The clever thing to do. The words went through her like ice, quenching the storm within her.

'Kiss me...'

'Darius, wait...please wait...'

'I don't want to wait any more—Harriet, let me...'

She drew back to meet his eyes, and what he saw in her cooled his ardour as mere words could never have done.

'This wasn't part of the bargain,' she said calmly. 'Friends, remember?'

'The bargain,' he said slowly. 'Ah, yes, the bargain. How could I have forgotten?'

'Exactly. You, of all people, should know about bargains.' As she said it she even managed a faint smile. 'Let's not complicate things by breaking ours.'

She could feel him shaking but he brought himself under control and stepped away.

'You're right, of course. I'll say goodnight...er...sleep well. I'll see you tomorrow.'

The door closed behind him, too quietly to hear, and then there was only darkness.

It was a long night. Darius spent it trying to order his thoughts, dismayed that they were suddenly rebellious, going their own way instead of obeying him as in the past.

Now he was alone he could admit that he was troubled by

what he'd learned that night. How painful Harriet's secrets must be for her to conceal them so determinedly. How sad must be her inner life. And he'd imagined that he knew her.

She had come into his arms, physically and, he'd hoped, emotionally, only for that hope to be dashed when she'd hastily retreated. The message was clear. Briefly she'd weakened, but then her husband's ghost had waked and that was the end. As, perhaps, it would always be.

He opened his window and stood listening to faint noises from next door. Her movements sounded restless, but what was she thinking? And would she ever tell him?

After a while he heard her window close, and then there was nothing to do but go to bed.

Harriet arose next morning with her mind made up. Cool, calm and collected, that was it. But also with a touch of their usual humour, to emphasise that nothing had changed.

In contrast to her glamour of last night, she donned a pair of functional jeans and a plain blouse. Her reflection stared back at her, asking if she really wanted this no-nonsense look when she could have something more enjoyable?

But I can't! It's a trap. No-nonsense suits me fine!

Not any longer. Never mind, it would have to do.

A waiter served breakfast in her room, and as he retreated Darius appeared at the door with a bread roll in one hand and a coffee in the other.

'Glad to see you up,' he said cheerfully. 'I was afraid the evening might have tired you too much.'

'I'm always up with the lark,' she assured him. 'Sit down. I'll be ready in a moment. I've packed up the jewellery ready to go back,' she said, indicating the box. 'Perhaps you'd better check it.'

Looking intent, Darius fingered the contents of the box until he came to the diamond pendant, which he lifted out.

'Not this,' he said. 'It's yours.'

'But it can't be. You hired this stuff.'

'Everything else, yes, but—oh, dear, did I forget to mention that I bought this one?'

'You certainly did.'

'Well, it's done now. Put it away safely.'

His expression was too innocent to be convincing, and she stared at him, open-mouthed with disbelief.

'Who do you think you're kidding?' she demanded.

His face was full of wicked delight. 'Not you, obviously.'

'You deceived me.'

'Yes, and I made a pretty good job of it too,' he said, defiantly unrepentant.

'You know I wouldn't have let you buy me anything as expensive as this.'

'Ah, well, I'm not used to people telling me what they'll let me do. It doesn't suit my autocratic, overbearing nature. I just do what I want and they have to put up with it. So there you are.' He assumed a grim expression. 'Put up with it.'

'You…you…'

He sighed. 'I know it's a great burden, but you'll learn to endure it.'

'It's…it's so beautiful,' she sighed. 'But you shouldn't have done it.'

'Don't tell me what I should and shouldn't do.'

'Yes, but—'

'Stop arguing. That's an order.'

It might be an order but it was delivered with a grin that made her heart turn over.

'Stop bullying me,' she demanded.

His grin broadened. 'I shall bully you if I want to. Now, put it away safely and don't lose it, otherwise I shall have to bully you even more by buying another.'

She ducked her head quickly so that he shouldn't see she was on the verge of tears.

Darius drank his coffee and went downstairs to pay the bill, congratulating himself on having tricked her into accepting his gift without risking the emotion that would have made her reject it.

When he returned she was on the phone to Phantom.

'I'm coming home, darling—see you later today—'

But by now Darius had himself in hand and could cope.

A car took them to the airport, where they boarded the helicopter and were soon soaring to the south and over the ocean, where the brilliant sun made the little waves sparkle.

'I love this time of year,' Harriet said, looking down to where Herringdean was just coming into view. 'The island is at its best.'

'I don't suppose you get called out on the lifeboat so often,' Darius observed.

'It depends. There aren't so many storms, but the fine weather tempts more people out in boats, so things still happen.'

Now they were crossing the coastline, covering the island until they reached the far side, and there below was the beach where they had first met.

'Look who I can see,' Darius said.

'Phantom!' she cried joyfully.

They could just make out the dog racing madly along the beach in pursuit of a ball thrown by a middle-aged woman, bringing it back to her, begging for it to be thrown again, which it always was.

'That's my neighbour, Jenny Bates,' Harriet said. 'She's wonderful with him. Hey, what's he doing now?'

Suddenly Phantom had changed course and raced into the sea. Mrs Bates ran to the water's edge and called him but he took no notice.

'Oh, no!' Harriet wailed.

'He'll be all right,' Darius said. 'He's swum often enough.'

'Yes, when I was with him. But without me he'll do something idiotic like going too far. Oh, look how far out he is! *Come back, you stupid dog!*'

'Land as close to the beach as you can,' Darius told the pilot quickly.

Down they went, finishing in almost the same place as on that first day, a lifetime ago, leaping out and running down onto the beach where Mrs Bates was wailing, 'I can't swim, I'm sorry—he's never done that before—'

'No problem,' Darius said. 'I'll go and—'

He'd been about to say that he would go after Phantom, but Harriet was way ahead of him, powering her way through the waves, calling Phantom urgently. He heard her and looked around, woofed in delight and began to paddle back to her. They met in deep water, greeting each other ecstatically with much crying and barking.

Darius remained where he was, knowing he wasn't needed.

As they emerged from the water Phantom recognised him, yelped joyfully and began to charge up the beach, spraying water everywhere. Quick as a flash, Harriet hurled herself onto the hound, taking him down to the sand.

'Oh, no, you don't,' she said breathlessly. 'Let the poor man have at least one suit that you don't ruin.' She looked up at Darius. 'You'd better run for it. I can't hold him much longer. Hurry up! Go quickly. Thank you for a lovely time, but go before he gets away from me. *Go!*'

There was nothing for it but to do as she said, so he returned to the helicopter. As it took off he looked down and discovered that history was repeating itself in that she was totally absorbed in Phantom, without even a glance to spare for himself.

It was only when he reached home he discovered that he still had her luggage. Briefly, he considered returning it in person, but settled for sending it in a taxi. He knew if he took it himself she would greet him politely while longing for him to be gone so that she could be alone with the one she really cared about.

And he couldn't face that. He could have dealt with her hostility, but her cool politeness would flatten him.

Coward, he thought wryly.

Amos would be ashamed of him.

But Amos could go and jump in the lake.

For a while things seemed peaceful. Harriet slipped back into her old routine, bathing in the mornings, sometimes seeing Darius on the beach for a few minutes, chatting about nothing much, cracking a few jokes before saying a polite goodbye.

One evening, while she was working late in her shop, a knock at the door made her look up and see him through the glass. She unlocked the door.

'Sorry, sir, we're closed for business,' she said cheekily.

'Thanks for the welcome. Hiya, Phantom. Careful not to knock any of these antiques around.'

'He doesn't need you to tell him to behave perfectly,' she said indignantly. 'He's always perfect.'

'Sure, that's why you pinned him to the ground when we landed.'

'Oh, well, that was different. What brings you here at this hour?'

'I'll be honest; I have an ulterior motive. And don't say it.'

'Say what?' she asked innocently.

'That I never do anything without an ulterior motive.'

'I wasn't going to say that.'

'No, but you were thinking it.'

'Very perceptive of you. All right, what's the ulterior motive?'

He held up his mobile phone.

'The kids call me every evening and they always ask to talk to you. I have to invent excuses why you're not there.'

'But surely they don't think we're living together?'

'Well...no, but they're surprised that you're never around.'

'But when they call tonight I will be around?' she hazarded.

'Exactly.'

'Unless I make a run for it.'

'You're too good a friend to do that.'

Before she could answer, the phone rang. Darius answered and his face lit up.

'Frankie, lovely to hear from you, darling. What have you been doing today?'

Harriet studied his face, taking in its warmth and pleasure. Her resolution to keep him at a polite distance was fading with every moment.

'What's that?' Darius asked. 'Harriet? Well...I'm not sure if...' He looked at her with pleading eyes. 'I'll see if she's here,' he said. 'I'm just going looking now.'

Silently, he mouthed, *Please*. Harriet relented and took the phone.

'Hi, Frankie! Boy, am I glad you called and gave me a chance to sit down! Your dad and I are working our socks off. I've just had a delivery at my shop and he's helping me unpack and put things away—he's doing very well.'

From the other end of the phone Darius could hear his little girl chuckling. He grinned.

'Yes, I'm really making him work,' Harriet said. 'He's surprisingly good. Let's face it, he looks like a wimp—oh, dear, I shouldn't have said that. If you could see how he's glaring at me—'

'I'm not,' Darius said indignantly.

'Anyway, he's not as much of a wimp as he looks. He can manage heavy weights—much to my surprise—'

Darius's indignation had faded and he was looking at her with resigned amusement. She laughed back at him, sending a silent message. *That'll teach you!* And receiving his message in return. *Just you wait!*

Harriet rattled away for a while, enjoying the sound of Frankie's delight. Then Mark took over, wanting to know if she'd been sailing. She'd taken her little yacht out only that morning and had plenty to tell him. It was a happy conversation.

At last she handed the phone back to Darius.

'It's a conspiracy,' he told his son. 'She's as bad as you are, or you're as bad as she is. I'm not sure which.'

Sounding relaxed and happy, he bid his children goodnight, then turned to her, laughing and exasperated in equal measure.

'Harriet, you little wretch! What are you trying to do to me? Wimp, indeed!'

'Shame!' she soothed him. 'All those hours spent in the gym, for nothing.'

'All right, enjoy your laugh. I suppose I asked for it.

And thank you. You did far more than I hoped for.' He looked around at the large boxes. 'You really have just had a delivery, haven't you?'

'Yes, a big one. Hey, what are you doing?'

'Well, I've got to prove I'm not a wimp, haven't I?' he said, beginning to unpack. 'Call it my gratitude.'

He wouldn't let her refuse, but worked for two hours fetching, carrying, lifting weights, finally breathing out hard and saying, 'I'm ready for a drink. Come on.'

The glass of ale in the pub that followed was in the same spirit of cheerful friendliness, and when they finally said goodnight she was able to feel confident that she'd successfully returned their relationship to safe territory.

She was to discover her mistake.

It was three days before she saw him again, racing towards her on the beach as she and Phantom emerged from the water, seizing her shoulders as soon as he reached her.

'You've got to help me,' he said. 'I know you won't want to but—'

'Why wouldn't I want to?'

'Well, I never stop asking for things, do I? It's always you giving and me taking—'

'Darius, calm down and tell me what it is.'

'Mary called me. The kids can't stay with their gran; she's gone down with a bug. It's not serious but they have to leave, and they want to come here.'

'Of course they want to be with you.'

'Yes, but Mary will only agree if you're part of the deal. I reckon it's really you they want to see rather than me.'

'Nonsense, you're their father.'

'Yes, but I'm still learning. Mary relies on you. If you don't say yes, *she* won't say yes. Please, Harriet.'

It was unfair of him, she thought, to look at her like that. How could she be sensible in the face of that imploring gaze, reminding her of his nicer side—the one that brought her dangerously close to falling in love?

'Of course I'll help you,' she said, 'as long as we agree beforehand what we're going to—'

She stopped as his cellphone had rung.

'Mary?' he said urgently. 'Yes, I've asked her and she's agreeable. It's going to be all right—what's that?—she's right here.' He handed her the phone.

'Harriet?' said Mary's urgent voice. 'Oh, thank heavens. We've got a disaster on our hands but I know you can take care of it.'

'Calm down; I'll be glad to help, and I'm sure they'll love the island.'

'Oh, yes, if you could have heard them talking after you spoke to them the other day. All I need to know is that you'll be there.'

'And I will.'

'They're well-behaved children. You won't have any trouble making them go to bed at the right time, and they're not picky eaters—'

'Mary, hang on, I didn't mean—'

But it was too late. With mounting dismay, Harriet realised that Mary had assumed that she was living with Darius and would be there for the children all the time.

'You don't understand,' she said frantically. 'I'm not actually—'

But she was watching Darius, and what she saw checked her. He'd followed her thoughts and was silently begging her not to destroy his hope.

'Not what?' Mary asked.

'I'm not—' She could tell that he was holding his breath. 'Not…not a very good cook,' she floundered.

'That's all right,' Mary assured her cheerfully. 'He says Kate's a terrific cook. All I'm asking you to do is be nice to them, and I know you will because—'

Harriet barely heard the rest. Dismayed, she realised that she'd committed herself to moving in with him, living close to him day and night, unable to escape the attraction that threatened to overwhelm her.

She'd been caught unawares, but now it was done and it was too late to undo. She could never bring herself to kill the blazing hope she could see in him. Dazed, she bid Mary farewell, handed over the phone and wandered to the water's edge.

What have I done? she whispered to herself. *Whatever have I done?*

Then she heard him calling her name, and turned to see him following her. The next moment he'd flung his arms around her.

'Thank you!' he said. *'Thank you!'*

He didn't try to kiss her, just held her with hands that gripped so tight it was almost painful. But she didn't even think of escape. There was a sweetness in his passionate gratitude that made her heart beat faster.

He drew back and she almost gasped at the sight of his face, lined with emotion, confusion, anguish and a kind of fierce joy that he himself didn't truly believe existed.

'Thank you,' he whispered again. 'Thank you, thank you.'

Now she knew what she'd done, and nothing in the world would ever make her regret it.

'I'm going to collect them in London tomorrow,' he said. 'Will you come with me?'

'If I can. I'll have to call the lifeboat station so that they've got a replacement on call. I'll do it now.'

At the station she was assured that there was no problem. There were plenty of volunteers to fill her place.

'It doesn't give you much time to move in,' Darius said, 'but I'll help you. And don't worry about anything. I know you didn't mean to live there but you can make everything just as you like it. Your word will be law, and you can choose your room. I won't trouble you, my word on it, and if you—'

'Stop, stop!' she said, laughing and touching his lips gently. 'You're babbling.'

He removed her fingers, but not before laying the lightest possible kiss on them, just enough to be felt, not enough for offence.

'I can't help it,' he said humbly. 'It matters so much, I can't risk anything going wrong.'

'Nothing's going to go wrong,' she promised. 'Now, we have a lot of work to do.'

'Yes, let's make a start. And you.' This last was addressed to Phantom, who'd nudged his hand.

'He's included?' Harriet asked eagerly.

'You don't think I'd leave him out, do you? The kids will love him. Now I come to think of it, he's almost more essential than you are.'

She chuckled. 'I think so too. Let's go.'

As they walked home his business side reasserted itself.

'What about your shop? You'll hardly have any time there for the next few weeks.'

'My assistant is reliable, and there's a temporary worker I sometimes use. She's very good.'

'Fine, hire her full-time at my expense. I pay her wages, is that clear? No argument.'

'I wasn't going to give you one,' she said. 'You're not the only one who can do business.'

She danced ahead of him, whistling.

CHAPTER TEN

HARRIET arranged the extra worker as soon as she got home, while Darius called Kate to alert her about Harriet's arrival.

They spent the rest of the day moving her things into Giant's Beacon. Kate ceremoniously showed her round the four available bedrooms, promising to get to work on whichever Harriet chose.

'You'll probably prefer the one at the end of the corridor,' Darius suggested, bland-faced.

It was certainly the most 'proper' room, being furthest from his, and having a lock on the door. It was also extremely ugly.

The nicest room was at the front of the house, just above the front door. There were two bay windows, a thick, newly laid carpet and a large comfortable-looking bed.

It was also directly opposite Darius's room.

'I wouldn't choose this if I were you,' Darius said. 'It's much too close to that fellow, and I've heard he's a bad character. Give him a wide berth.'

'And you'd know him better than anyone else, I suppose,' she riposted.

'Definitely. You shouldn't even have been shown this room, even though it's the most comfortable, and lovely in the mornings when the sun comes in.'

'Yes, I noticed it was facing the dawn.'

'But it doesn't have a lock on the door,' he pointed out.

'Ah, but he's promised not to trouble me. If he keeps his word, why would I need a lock?'

'That's very true.'

'And if he doesn't—I'll set Phantom on him.'

'There's a threat to frighten a man.'

'So I think—' She threw herself onto the soft mattress, and Phantom jumped up beside her. 'Yes, I think we'll have this one.' She turned to her companion. 'Do you agree?'

Woof!

'Then if everyone's satisfied,' Darius said, 'we'll call it a day, and be ready to leave early tomorrow.'

The helicopter was there on the dot, sweeping them off to the airport near London. From there a car took them to the house where the children were staying. Mark and Frankie were watching from the window, and yelled with delight when they saw them.

'Dad! You came!' Frankie cried.

'But of course I came. I said I would.'

They didn't reply, but Harriet wondered how often in the past he hadn't been there when he said he would.

The housekeeper appeared, saying that their hostess wouldn't come downstairs because of her illness, but she sent her thanks and best wishes. Darius returned a message of condolence, and they were ready to go.

As they left the house Harriet happened to notice the children exchanging glances, and was almost certain that she heard Mark whisper, 'I told you she'd come.'

On the journey home they made her talk about Herringdean, yearning for the moment when they could look down at it from high in the air. When that moment finally came they were speechless, gazing open-mouthed at so much beauty. Darius, watching them, understood.

'That's what I thought when I first saw it,' he said. 'The loveliest place in the world.'

They nodded agreement, but Harriet detected a slight bafflement in their manner. Their father had actually said that? Who was he trying to kid?

At last it was time to land and make their way to Giant's Beacon. As she had expected, their first meeting with Phantom was joyful. Since he asked nothing better than to be the centre of attention all the time and they had lots of attention to give, they forged an instant three-way friendship.

After supper she and Kate saw them to bed with the promise of plenty of action next day. They were already yawning and climbed into bed without argument.

Downstairs, Darius poured her a glass of wine and raised his own glass in salute.

'To you,' he said. 'Without you, none of this would be happening.'

'But it is happening. Now it's up to you to make the best of it.'

'Did you see their faces when I told them I felt the same as they when I first saw Herringdean? They didn't really believe I could feel that way.' He added wryly, 'Any more than you did.'

'I wish you'd stop brooding about that. It was a lifetime ago. You're not the same man.'

'Maybe not,' he murmured. 'But who am I now?'

'You'll find that out with them.'

'And you?'

'No. This is you and them. I'm not really a part of it.'

'That's not true and you know it,' he said quietly.

Suddenly she was faced with a dilemma. His words offered her the chance to turn the conversation in a direction that tempted her. Try as she might to stop her heart inclining towards him, it seemed to have a life of its own, beating more intensely when he was near, bringing her alive in his presence in a way that wasn't true at any other time. A little cleverness, a little scheming, and she could secure him. It would be so easy, if only—

If only she could bring herself to settle for second best, for a marriage in which she gave love in return only for gratitude.

'Why did you sigh?' he asked. 'Did I offend you by saying that?'

'No, of course not.'

'I really forced you here against your will, didn't I? I'm sorry.'

'There's nothing to be sorry for. Stop being so gloomy. Now, I'm going to take Phantom out for a walk before I go to bed.'

'I'll come with you.'

'Better not,' she said quickly. 'He wants me to himself for a while. Goodnight.'

She slipped away before he could say any more, escaping from the danger that always hovered in his presence these days, hurrying out of the house, signalling Phantom to follow her. Darius watched them run away in the moonlight, and only when they were out of sight did he climb the stairs to find two little faces looking down at him.

'Dad, *Dad!*'

'What are you two doing up? You should be asleep.'

'Harry's gone,' Frankie wailed. 'She took Phantom with her.'

'Don't panic. They've just gone for a walk. They'll be back.'

'Promise!' she demanded.

'Word of honour. And if she doesn't I'll go and fetch them. Now, back to bed.'

They vanished obediently and he, being naïve, assumed they had obeyed him. It was only later, as he strolled in the garden watching for Harriet's return, that he realised they were looking out of the window over his head.

'Is she coming yet?' Mark called.

Darius was about to admonish them when he had the strangest sensation that Harriet was there, reading his mind, shaking her head in disapproval. Enlightenment dawned.

'Come on down and we'll wait together,' he called back.

They darted away, appearing in the garden a moment later. Kate brought out milkshakes and they sat around a small table, chatting to pass the time. Darius described his first encounter with Phantom. Once, the thought of anyone, even—or especially—his own children—knowing about that undignified incident would have filled him with horror. Now, he found himself describing it in detail, relishing their shrieks of laughter.

Harriet would have been proud of him, he felt.

'Perhaps we should go with her next time,' Frankie suggested.

'You don't have to keep guard over her,' Darius said. 'She's not going to run away.'

'Really? She'll stay with us for ever and ever?'

'That's for her to say,' Darius said quietly.

A mysterious understanding was creeping over him. Like himself, they had seen Harriet in a light that set her apart from everyone else, as though she possessed a special power that acted like a shield against all the evil of the world. Those she defended were safe. Those she loved were fortunate beyond their dreams.

The difference between them was that they had seen at once what he had taken time to understand. And that delay might be his undoing. But for now he must profit by her influence to find the right words for his children's questions. He crossed his fingers, hoping against hope for wisdom.

But before he could speak Harriet again intervened to save him.

'Here she is,' Frankie cried, bounding up and pointing to two figures emerging from the trees.

She and Mark made off at top speed and in the riot of noisy delight nobody noticed Darius closing his eyes and thanking a merciful fate. When he was calm again he strolled towards her, calling, 'Nice to see you back.'

Harriet smiled at him. 'Nice to be back,' she said.

His eyes held hers. 'Really?'

'Yes, really. Right, you kids. Bed.'

When that job was done she leaned against the wall, yawning. 'I'm nodding off right here.'

'Go and get some sleep, because you're going to need it.'

'You too. Goodnight.'

Harriet slept until the early hours, then got up and glanced out of the window. From here she could just see a glow of light that she knew came from Darius's office.

Throwing on her dressing gown, she slipped downstairs. From behind the door she could hear him on the phone.

'I accessed the website half an hour ago and there's no doubt—I know how to fight this—I've already put things in place that'll make them think twice—don't worry, I've got it in hand.'

He sounded almost like the man she'd heard before vowing, 'No mercy', but she sensed something different. The cruelty had gone from his voice and only the determination remained.

As he hung up she opened the door and found him staring at the screen. He looked round and smiled wanly.

'Don't you ever sleep?' she asked.

'I'm trying to catch up at night so that I can be free during the day. There are things I still have to do.'

'You poor soul. Can I do anything to help?'

'I'd be glad of a coffee.'

She disappeared into the kitchen, returning with a full mug a few minutes later, only to find him dozing. She set down the mug and laid a gentle hand on his shoulder, so that he awoke at once, looking up at her with a faint smile. She had never seen him so vulnerable, never been so dangerously close to loving him.

'I'm going to do it,' he said. 'You'll be proud of me, teacher.'

'I was proud of you tonight,' she said. 'When I saw you sitting outside with them, cracking jokes. You must have been telling them a great story to make them laugh like that.'

'Yes, they really enjoyed hearing how their dad looked like a total prat.'

'I don't believe you said anything like that.' When Darius simply grinned she said, 'Well, go on, I can't stand the curiosity. Tell, tell!'

'It was about our first meeting—the way Phantom flattened me on the sand. I thought they'd enjoy it, and they did.'

'You actually managed to tell *that* story?' she breathed in astonishment and admiration. 'How come?'

'You told me to,' he said simply.

'I never—' She stopped. 'When did I?'

'There and then.'

'But I wasn't there.'

'Yes, you were. You were right there with me. You always are. Even when you're not there, you *are* there. Didn't you know?'

'No,' she murmured.

His gaze intensified. 'I guess there are a lot of things you don't know.'

'I guess there are.'

'I'm glad I'm not the only one who's confused.'

Everything was in a whirl. He was telling her something she longed with all her heart to hear, to believe; telling her not with words but with his eyes, with his hesitant tone, with his uncertainty that seemed to say everything was in her hands.

Playing for time, she said lightly, 'The great financier is never confused.'

'That's what *he* used to think,' he agreed. 'So when the confusion came he didn't know how to cope with it.'

A soft buzz came from the screen.

'You've got an email,' she said. 'I'm going back to bed. So should you. Get some sleep.'

She slipped away and ran back to her room, telling herself that she was glad of the interruption that had saved her from saying and doing things that she would regret.

If she tried really hard she might even manage to believe that.

Mark and Frankie were instinctively happy outdoors. Town life bored them, and escaping to the island lifted them to seventh heaven. They revelled in the visit to Harriet's little yacht, and the trip out to sea, gaining particular pleasure from their father's ignorance, even greater than their own, and the way he addressed Harriet as 'Captain'. Several times Harriet caught them exchanging knowing glances.

At home she took charge, banishing Darius to the office to catch up with his work while she and Kate saw to supper.

'Isn't Dad having supper with us?' Mark asked.

'The poor man's got to do a little work,' Harriet said. 'Last night he worked late so that he could spend the day with you. Now, I'll take his supper in to him.'

'Are you and Dad going to get married?' Frankie asked.

'It's much too soon to think of anything like that,' Harriet said quickly. 'We're just friends for now, and we're not rushing it. Don't mention it to him.'

Frankie nodded wisely. Harriet was left staring at Darius's office door. He'd been closing it when Frankie asked her question, and although Harriet tried to believe that he couldn't have heard anything she'd noticed the way the door was suddenly still for a moment, before being shut.

At the end of the evening he emerged to join them for a walk with Phantom, and perhaps only Harriet noticed that he was unusually quiet. Later, when the children had gone to bed and the house was quiet, it wasn't a surprise when he knocked on her bedroom door.

'I just wanted to say I'm sorry that Frankie embarrassed you,' he said, coming in. 'She's too young to understand that…well, things have to happen slowly.'

'You're right,' she said. 'Going slowly can save you from a lot of mistakes.'

'Does that mean anything special?' he asked, almost daring to hope.

'I guess it does.' She fell silent.

'Harriet,' he whispered, 'don't shut me out. Not any more.'

She sighed. 'I rushed into marriage with Brad…I was so young…ah, well…'

'Don't stop there,' he begged. 'Talk to me. You keep everything bolted and barred, and you shouldn't.'

'I know. I don't mean to but I've hidden the truth for so

long that it's hard to change now. My neighbours think we were the perfect couple, and that's what I wanted them to think. I'd have been ashamed for them to know the truth. I loved Brad so much but he…well, he just took my love for granted and did as he liked.'

'Go on,' he said gently. 'Harriet, please tell me everything. You know so much about me, but you hide from me and keep me on the outside.'

She drew away suddenly and went to the window, throwing back her head, breathing harshly. She felt as though she were being torn in two directions. It had taken her so long to reach this point and now her courage was failing her. She saw Darius watching her closely, with an expression so gentle that she reached out to him without even realising.

At once he went to her. 'Tell me,' he said again. 'Don't shut me out. If only I could make you understand how important it is.'

'Why?' she whispered.

He answered by laying his lips tenderly on hers, leaving them for just a moment.

'Can you understand now?' he asked.

She searched his face. 'I'm not sure. I'm so confused.'

'Trust me, Harriet. That's all I ask.'

She rested her head against him. 'Our marriage was a mistake. I rushed into love, and when it went wrong I wouldn't admit to myself that he wasn't the man I'd thought. I don't think he was ever really faithful to me, but nobody else knew because he was away so often.

'In the end he left me for a woman he'd met in America. He went to live with her over there, and they died together in a car crash. I still have the last letter he wrote me, demanding a quick divorce because his lover was pregnant. That really hurt because I'd always wanted children and he was the one who insisted on waiting.

'It's strange, but after what he did to me, the thing I'll really never be able to forgive him for is the way he abandoned Phantom. That poor dog adored him. When Brad was away he'd sit at the window, watching and watching until he returned. Then he'd go mad with happiness.

'I loved Phantom too, but I always knew I was second best to him. And when Brad said he was leaving him behind—I couldn't believe he could be so cruel. It was *her* fault. She didn't want him, so Brad simply tossed him out of his life.'

Darius uttered one word, vulgar and full of feeling.

'That's what I said,' Harriet agreed.

'I'll never forget the day he left. Phantom watched him loading his things into the car. He began to wail, then to howl, and he ran after Brad and tried to get between him and the front door. I'll swear he knew what was happening, and was begging not to be left behind.

'Brad pushed him aside and shouted at him. Then he went out and got into the car. Phantom followed, but suddenly everything seemed to drain out of him, and he just sat there in the road while the car vanished. I hated Brad at that moment. I could forgive him for leaving me, but not for breaking that poor creature's heart.

'After that, Phantom sat at the window every day, waiting for his return. Then one day he didn't go to the window, but just lay there staring into space. He knew it was final.

'I've tried to make it up to him. I tell him how much I love him, and I promise that I'll never, never desert him or let him down in any way.'

'Harriet, you're talking about him as though he was a person.'

'I suppose that's how I think of him, except that he's more loyal and loving than any human being. I think he's happy with me now, but I wonder if he still mourns Brad.'

'Perhaps that depends on you,' Darius said carefully. 'If he can tell that *you* still mourn Brad—'

'But I don't,' she said, a little too quickly, he thought. 'He's a part of my life that's over. I love Phantom for his own sake. How could I not love him when he's so lovable?'

'And when he reminds you of Brad,' Darius said. 'Are you sure you aren't hiding from the truth, just a little? Are you really over him?'

'That was another life, another world. It doesn't even feel like me any more.'

That was a clever reply, he thought wryly, because it sounded like a denial without actually being one.

'What about this world?' he asked, choosing his words carefully.

'This is the one that matters. I know that. It's just so hard to know where I belong in it. Sometimes I feel I never will know.' She searched his face.

'I can help you there,' he said, laying his mouth over hers and murmuring through the kiss. 'This is where you belong, in my arms, in my heart.'

She silenced him with the soft pressure of her own mouth, reaching up to caress his face before sliding one hand behind his head. She'd fought so hard to cling onto caution, but now she banished it without another thought. Whatever pain the future might hold, she would risk it in return for the beauty of this moment.

When she felt him drawing her to the bed she went willingly. Now everything in her wanted what was about to happen. Fear and mistrust were set aside as she felt a new self coming to life within her, and knew that this was the self that was always meant to be, a self that could yield joyfully to passion, but for whom tenderness mattered as much, or even more.

For, dazzling as was the physical pleasure, it was the look in his eyes that made her sigh with happiness as he brought her to the moment they both longed for. And afterwards it was the strength of his arms around her that carried her safely back to earth.

Now, at last, she knew where she belonged.

CHAPTER ELEVEN

HARRIET need not have been worried about the visit. It was blessed from the start by the fact that both children were instinctively at home in the country. Sailing, bathing on the beach, running through fields and trees with Phantom, trips around the island to small villages and communities—all this was their idea of heaven.

In only one respect was the holiday less than perfect. It lacked what they most longed for, and that was to see Harriet called out on a lifeboat rescue.

She'd obtained permission for them to visit the station where her friends greeted them jovially, and showed them around, including a moored lifeboat. But no emergency turned up, and the excitement they longed for failed to materialise.

It was time for the Ellarick Regatta. For the last week the hotels had been filling up, the island was full of visitors and the port was brilliant with flags. Mark and Frankie each had a copy of the programme, which never left them.

'How many races are you in?' Mark had demanded, studying the lists although he knew them by heart.

'It depends,' Harriet said. 'If I get eliminated in an early heat I won't go on to the next, but if I finish in the first three I'll go on to the next heat, and the next and maybe even the final.'

'And then you'll win the small boat trophy,' Frankie said triumphantly. 'Like before.'

'How did you know?'

'It's listed here,' Mark said, showing her. 'You've won once, and come second three times. Did you get a big prize?'

'I got a trophy. I keep it in the shop.'

'Then it's time we all saw it,' Darius announced.

They had a jolly expedition to the shop that, as Harriet had said, sold as many gifts as antiques, and at this time of year was full of souvenirs of the regatta. Darius kitted them out with T-shirts, plus anything else that took their fancy, and they ended the day in an ice cream bar.

That night Harriet went to bed early as she had to be up in the early hours. The children bid her a formal goodnight and blew her kisses before retreating. Darius saw her to her door.

'Aren't you coming in to tuck me up?' she asked innocently.

'You need to be at your best tomorrow. Go to bed, get some sleep,' he commanded.

'If you say so. Just one goodnight kiss—'

She took possession of his mouth before he could protest, kissing him softly, then with more vigour, then fiercely.

'Harriet, you're not being fair,' he murmured desperately.

'So who's fair?' she whispered back.

'I'm trying to protect you from distractions—'

'When I need your protection I'll ask for it. Now, come inside and stop arguing.'

This was another new person, one who could shamelessly demand a man's attentions while equally shamelessly offering her own. No, not offer her own, insist on her own, for he was trying to be virtuous and resist her, and she wasn't going to have that.

It was a week since they had found each other, and she had spent every moment of that week wanting to enjoy him again, that might have embarrassed her if she hadn't known he felt exactly the same. They'd been careful. The need to put the children first had meant there were fewer chances than they might have hoped. But tonight was a chance she was determined to seize—whatever nonsense he might talk.

When at last they lay dozing together, he murmured, 'Now you must go out and win.'

'But I did win,' she whispered. 'Just now. Didn't you notice?'

'I kind of thought I was the winner.'

'We'll call it a tie.' Her lips twitched. 'But I'm not sharing the trophy.'

'That's all right. We'll compete for another one in the next round.' He kissed her. 'And now I'm leaving—'

'Are you?' she said, moving her hand.

'Yes, you little wretch—Harriet, don't do that, it isn't fair—'

'I'm not trying to be fair—'

'I know what you're trying to do—*Harriet!*'

After that there was silence for a long time. Then he gathered his energy enough to say, 'Now I really am going so that you can go to sleep. You have to be at your best tomorrow. You've got to triumph in that race and go into the next round and win there, and we're all going to be there when you get the trophy. I'll be cheering and the kids will be cheering—'

'Ah, yes, the children,' she sighed. 'It's all for them. Don't let's forget that.'

Rejoicing in the pleasure of this wonderful time, she

often forgot the conversation she'd overheard, suggesting that Darius had another motive for securing her. Not only the passion they shared, but also the sense of being close in heart and mind, rescued her from fear. All would be well, she was increasingly sure of it.

From the door he blew her a kiss and was gone.

In the early hours of next morning she was up with the lark, finding the taxi waiting at the door. By mutual agreement, Darius was remaining at home with the children rather than driving her.

Then the port came in sight, and she forgot everything but the excitement of the regatta. She got to work on her yacht, making sure everything was ready, then settled in, feeling herself become one with it.

Forty yachts were entered for the race, but only ten could compete at any one time, so it began with heats. Some of the crowd watched from the shore, but the view was better from the large ferries that had positioned themselves out at sea, and Harriet knew that the three of them would be on one of these, eagerly watching for her.

They were off. She managed to keep ahead of most of the other boats, without actually getting into the lead. Halfway through the race she saw Darius and the children leaning over the railing of a ferry, cheering her. Inspired, she redoubled her efforts and managed to arrive second.

'That's it,' Darius said as they welcomed her ashore. 'You're in the next heat.'

'And next time you'll be first,' Mark said loyally.

'You'll show 'em,' Frankie cried.

And she did. Whether it was the sense of a loyal family rooting for her, or whether it was simply her time, she won the next heat, came second in the next, and won the final race. When she came ashore the band was playing as she went up to the dais to receive the trophy. There were photographs to be taken, herself holding up her prize, with Frankie and Mark one each side, then Frankie and Mark holding the prize. Darius was in some of the pictures too, but usually in the background, rather to her disappointment.

The day ended in a restaurant, being ecstatically toasted not only by the family but by her many friends. Then home to be toasted again.

Darius ended the evening, as he always did, at the computer, catching up with the work he'd been unable to do during the day. He looked worn out, she realised. With every day he seemed to get less and less sleep. She crept away and left him.

He came to her two hours later. 'I was afraid you might have gone to sleep by now,' he said, closing the door behind him.

'I'm just about to.' She yawned theatrically. 'I simply can't keep awake.'

Laughing, he took her into his arms. 'Let's see if I can help you find sweet dreams.'

She slipped her arms about his neck. 'Hmm, let me think about that.'

'Don't think too hard,' he murmured, dropping his head so that his lips were against her neck.

'You're a wicked man, you know that?'

'Would you like me to go away?'

'I'm not sure. Do that again and I'll decide.'

Their first love-making had been full of tender emotion, and because of that it had been perfect. Over the next few days, a new pleasure had revealed itself, love and laughter at the same time, and she discovered that its joy could be as great as any other. She hadn't known before that she could be a tease, but she was learning it now and revelling in the lesson.

He caressed her, watching her expression intently.

'Are you any closer to making your mind up?' he wanted to know.

'I'm not sure. Some things take longer to decide than others.' She stretched out luxuriously. 'But we have plenty of time.'

'Yes, all the time in the world,' he said with relish.

As he spoke he was drawing his fingers down her, touching lightly so she took a long breath as her desire rose.

'I've thought about nothing but this since last time,' he murmured. 'And the time before.'

'Neither have I. You're here now, and I'm going to enjoy every moment.'

'I intend to make sure you do—*what the blazes is that?*'

A shrill noise had rent the air, then again, and again and again.

'Oh, no,' Harriet groaned. 'That's my pager. I'm needed on the lifeboat. I've got to dash.'

'You're going to run away *now*?'

'I don't have any choice,' she cried, shoving him aside and making a grab for her clothes.

For a moment he was too stunned to speak, but lay on the bed, his heart pounding as he fought to bring himself under control. This couldn't be happening. It mustn't happen. To have the prize snatched from him as the climax mounted— to be defeated at the last moment and told to put up with it. His head was spinning.

'Bye,' she cried and headed for the door.

'Wait!' he cried, getting command of himself at the last minute, 'I'll drive you there.'

'I can't wait for you. I'm on my way.'

She was gone. A moment later, he heard her car start up.

Dazed, he wrenched on his clothes and went out into the corridor, to find his children already there.

'Dad, what's happened?' Mark demanded. 'There was a funny noise and Harry dashed off. She hasn't been called, has she?'

'That's right, she's on her way to the lifeboat station now.'

'Oh, wow!' Both children began to leap about. 'Let's go too, please, Dad.'

'They won't let us in. They're doing a serious job and we'd be in the way.'

'But we can watch from the shore and see the boat go out. Please, Dad, please, please, *please*.'

They were bouncing up and down, looking up at him beseechingly.

'All right,' he said, relenting. 'Get dressed fast.'

In ten minutes they were sweeping out of the drive. On the journey he switched on the car radio, tuned to the local station, that was carrying news about a small party out on a jaunt who'd sent a frantic radio message that their boat had sprung a leak.

By the time they arrived they were several minutes behind Harriet, who had completely vanished, but the station was buzzing with life. A crowd had gathered just outside, and they quickly joined it. A cheer rose as the lifeboat went down the slipway, hitting the water so that spray rose up high.

'Was it like this for you, Dad?' Mark breathed.

'I don't exactly know,' he said wryly. 'I wasn't here. I was a few miles out, going down for the third time.'

That was roughly how he felt right now. His mind told him that she'd had no choice but to leave and save others as she had saved him. He had no reasonable complaint.

But that was only his mind. The rest of him was complaining bitterly at losing the prize at the crucial moment.

She had laid in his arms, tender and sweet, giving him the look he loved, the one that said he could bring her a pleasure and happiness she'd never dreamed of before. That look had the power to open his heart, inviting her to reach out to him, as he reached out to her more with every day that passed.

Until now he'd shown his growing feelings through touch, waiting until he was sure of the right words. Since the night she'd confided in him he'd felt his defences collapse. The barrier of her husband's memory, once looming so high between them, no longer existed. She'd trusted and confided in a way he hadn't expected, filling him with happiness but also with a slight sense of guilt that he hadn't matched her openness with his own.

Honesty demanded that he admit he already knew the secret she was finally revealing, but he hadn't been able to bring himself to do it. It would involve telling her about his father's spies, and in her anger and dismay she might have laid some of the blame on himself. Not for the world would he risk damaging the bond between them. At least, not yet.

Soon he would be able to tell her of his feelings. It might even have been that night. But then—

He groaned. There were two Harriets—the passionate loving one, and the brave efficient one who put duty before everything. Tonight, the second one had taken over, leaving him stranded. Life with her would be more complex than he'd ever dreamed. Also more intriguing . That suggested an interesting future.

But tonight he was aching with frustration and thwarted feelings.

Hours passed. Occasionally someone would come out of

the station to brief the watchers on how things were going. So they knew that the lifeboat had reached its destination, rescued everyone safely, and was on its way back.

At last it appeared on the horizon, just visible in the faint gleam of the dawn. The children watched, thrilled, as it came closer and was hauled back up the slipway. When Harriet appeared they ran to greet her and be introduced to the rest of the crew. They were in seventh heaven.

'Gosh,' Mark exclaimed. 'Wasn't that the most wonderful thing that ever happened?'

'Oh, yes,' Darius said wryly. 'Wonderful.'

But his personal feelings vanished when he saw Harriet on the edge of total exhaustion.

'Let's get you home fast,' he said. 'Leave your car here; you're too tired to drive. I'll fetch it later. Let her have the back seat, kids, so that she can stretch out.'

She did manage to stretch out, falling asleep almost at once, and waking to find her head resting in Frankie's arms.

'We're home now,' the little girl said kindly. 'I'll help you to bed.'

With Kate's assistance, she did, finally emerging to where Mark and her father were waiting in the corridor.

'All right for me to go in?' Darius asked.

'Just for a moment,' she told him sternly. 'She needs to sleep.'

Darius gave her a comic salute. 'Yes, ma'am. Anything you say, ma'am.'

He vanished into Harriet's room too quickly to see his children stare at each other with an unmistakable message; Dad said *that*?

Going quietly to the bed, Darius whispered, 'Hello.'
Silence.

Leaning closer, he heard her faint breathing and realised that she was asleep.

'I guess Frankie was right to protect you,' he murmured. 'You need it sometimes. It's a pity about tonight because I was going to say…all sorts of things. Now they'll have to wait until the time is right.' He touched her face with gentle fingers. 'Let's hope that day comes soon.'

He kissed her softly, and left the room without her knowing that he'd been there.

The last few days of the holiday built on the success of the first week. Darius's relationship with his children was becoming everything he had hoped, and his manner towards Harriet was full of affection and gratitude.

'Without you, this would never work,' he told her. 'However much I want to, I can't spend all my time with them. I have to keep an eye on what's happening out there.'

'I know. You were up almost until dawn last night,' she said. 'I don't know how you manage to stay awake.'

'I don't always,' he said ruefully. 'Thank goodness for you distracting them. I swear if I nod off they barely notice.'

The end of the holiday was near. The four of them would fly to London, where the children would be reunited with Mary. After that, she hoped she and Darius would have a little time together before returning to Herringdean.

But the day before they were due to leave the financial world began to call to Darius more urgently. Hardly a minute passed without a text, an email or a call on his cellphone.

'Is it bad news?' she asked him urgently.

'Not bad, just interesting. It could go either way, depending on how I handle it. I think we need to change our plans.

It's best if you don't come to London after all. I'll have to stay there a few days, sort some things out. So I'll take the kids back to Mary and stay out of your hair for a while.' He grinned. 'You'll be glad to have a rest from me.'

'Of course I will,' she said in a dead voice. 'Who could think otherwise?'

The children complained bitterly about her not coming with them.

'I've got work to do,' she said cheerfully. 'It's time I took over the shop and I have to go to training sessions for the lifeboat.'

'But we will see you again?' Frankie urged.

'I'm sure you will. Who knows what's around the corner?'

She spoke brightly, but she couldn't help being glad Darius wasn't there to hear. She couldn't have helped watching for his reaction, and now something in her was warning her to expect the worst.

On the day she saw them off and stood looking up into the sky as the helicopter rose higher and higher, then swung away until it disappeared completely and the sky was empty but for a few seagulls.

How lonely it was now. After the pleasures of the last week, the quiet and emptiness were almost unbearable. Worse still was the fear that what had gone was gone for ever. He had said the news could be good, depending on how he handled it, and she guessed he would handle it with skill, perhaps ruthlessness. The 'no mercy' side of him would rise and take over again.

He would leave Herringdean, having no further use for it, or for her. He'd learned how to reach out to his children and he could carry those lessons forward without her help. He'd settle back in London, find a wife who suited him better, sell Herringdean and forget she existed.

And I should have known it would happen, she thought.
*All this time the truth has been staring me in the face, but
I wouldn't let myself see it.*

It was time to be sensible. She was good at that, she
reminded herself. She had a shop to see to, and Phantom
to look after. He was showing signs of depression now his
two adoring young friends had gone.

'People always go off and leave you, don't they?' she
said, caressing him. 'Well, not me. I'll always be here for
you. That's a promise.'

Moving back into her home, she filled up the time by
cleaning it. More time was occupied at the lifeboat station,
but mostly in training sessions. For some reason, very few
boats got into trouble.

Now she began to understand Mark and Frankie's frustration at the lack of action. Why couldn't people obligingly
get into danger so that she could have the satisfaction of
saving them? Not that she wanted anyone to suffer. She just
wanted to feel needed, and that was becoming hard.

For the first few days Darius called her regularly, but
the calls were always brief. Then they were replaced by
texts, friendly, cheerful but unrevealing. Exactly the kind
of message a man might send if he was easing his way out
of a relationship.

One evening she and Phantom went out for a long walk.
As she strolled back home a car passed her going in the
other direction, and slowed down. It was Walter.

'I just drove past your place,' he called, 'and there's a
fellow standing there.'

'Did you see who it was?' she asked eagerly.

'No, I wasn't that close, but he looked as if he was waiting for you.'

'Thanks, Walter.'

Her heart soaring, she sped away, racing Phantom until

her shop came in sight and she dashed around the corner, to where a man was walking impatiently up and down.

It was Amos Falcon.

CHAPTER TWELVE

'GOOD evening, Mrs Connor.'

Harriet wondered if she'd only imagined that he stressed 'Mrs' very slightly.

'Good evening, Mr Falcon. What a surprise. You didn't tell me you were coming.'

'It was a sudden decision. Aren't you going to invite me in?'

'Of course.'

She led him up to her apartment over the shop, keeping her hand on Phantom's collar, dreading that he might give one of his displays of friendliness. But she need not have feared. When they were inside, Phantom moved as far away from Amos as possible and sat huddled in a corner, eyeing him distrustfully.

When the door had shut, Harriet said, 'If you were hoping to see Darius—'

'I wasn't. I know he's in London. I've seen him several times in the last few days.' He was watching her face carefully, easily seeing that this disconcerted her. 'Did he not tell you that? Strange.'

On first finding him there she had remembered how pleasantly he'd spoken to her when they danced at the wedding. But now she saw that his smile was cold, and she remembered how Darius had described his father—ruthless, scheming, implacable; a man who was determined to make others do his will. She recalled too that Amos had chosen a wife for his son, and wondered uneasily what had brought him such a distance to see her.

'So you don't know what's been happening to him?' Amos said in a genial voice that struck a false note to her ears.

'I don't ask Darius about his business,' Harriet said. 'I doubt if I'd understand it, anyway.'

'Possibly, but when a man is taking hold of his problems and dealing with them successfully it's not hard to understand. Anyway, never mind that. You and I have things to discuss.'

'Coffee?' she asked politely.

'Thank you, I will. You know, I really took to you when we met before. You're an admirable young woman, not just because you helped save my son's life, but also because of the way you've built up this shop. It's worth a lot more than you'd think by just looking at the outside.'

'How do you know what it's worth?' she asked.

He shrugged. 'That kind of information isn't hard to come by. It belonged to your husband but he had very little time for it so the running of it fell to you. It was you who arranged the loans and made sure they were paid on time.'

'So you've been looking at my bank records?' she asked in outrage.

She knew that a man like this, who stood at the summit of the financial universe, would have no difficulty in accessing any figures that he wanted, yet the discovery that he'd had her investigated was a nasty shock that made her seethe.

'And I've been very impressed by what I found. You've turned this place into twice what it was before. I'm prepared to pay a high price for it.'

'It's not for sale.'

He gave a harsh chuckle. 'Of course it isn't. That's exactly what I expected you to say.'

'And I meant it.'

'Naturally. But you and I don't need to waste any time. We both know what the score is. You've gained a real influence over my son, but now that he's returning to his old life I don't want him harking back to you. The fight isn't over yet and he's going to need all his faculties to come out on top.'

Then Harriet did something that she did very rarely. She lost her temper, turning on him with such a look that he nearly backed away.

'Understand me,' she said. 'I will not discuss Darius with you. If he wants to consign me to the past then he can tell me himself, and I'll open my hands and let him go. I will not try to keep a stranglehold on him, and you don't have to buy me off. Is that clear?'

Amos Falcon's response was a genial smile that made her want to murder him.

'Perfectly clear and I respect your strength of mind, but you should allow me to show that respect by purchasing your shop at twice its value. You won't get such an offer again.'

'You're crazy,' she breathed. 'You think everyone's for sale.'

'No, I simply think you should be considering the long-term implications. After the appalling way your husband treated you, you should be protecting yourself.'

His words were like a douche of ice.

'The appalling way—? Darius told you about that?'

'Not at all. I told him.'

Suddenly the world had turned into a nightmare through which she could only stumble.

'You told—? When?'

'At the wedding. I discovered I knew rather more about you than he did, so I brought him up to date.'

Now she couldn't speak at all, only look at him from wide, horrified eyes.

'He was very chivalrous,' Amos went on. 'He said it was entirely a matter for you if you wanted to keep your secrets, which, of course, is right. But I think he was a little disturbed to discover that you'd been holding him off while pretending to be close to him.'

Harriet's head swam. There in her mind was the sweet moment when she'd confided in Darius what she'd told nobody else, meaning in this way to prove her trust in him.

But he'd known all the time, and never told her.

'Get out,' she breathed. 'Get out now, if you know what's good for you.'

'He doesn't,' said a voice from the door. 'He's never known what was good for him.'

Shocked, they both turned to see Darius standing there, a look of dark fury on his face.

'You heard her,' he told his father. 'Get out. Get off this island and don't ever come back.'

'What are you doing here?' Amos shouted.

'When I found out where you'd gone I came after you as fast as I could. I knew you'd try something like this. Luckily, I arrived in time to spike your guns.'

'I was only trying to do my best for you,' Amos growled. 'You've done so well these past few days.'

'Yes, I've put a lot of things right, not everything but enough to survive. And now I'm coming back here to stay. For good. I'm moving my centre of operations here permanently. From now on I'll operate out of Giant's Beacon, with the help of my wife.'

'Your wife!' Amos snapped. 'You mean you've asked her? Of all the damn fool—'

'No, I haven't asked her,' Darius said with a glance at Harriet. 'And after what you've told her I wouldn't give much for my chances. But I'm a man who doesn't give up. When I want something I keep on and on until I get it. *You* taught me that, and I was never more glad of a lesson in my life.

'It won't be easy. Why should any woman in her right mind want to marry into this family? But I'll keep going until she forgives me for keeping that little matter of her husband to myself, and understands that I can't live without her. Then, perhaps she'll take pity on me.'

Harriet tried to speak but she couldn't. Her eyes were blinded with tears and something was almost choking her.

'Now go,' Darius said quietly.

Amos knew when he was beaten. With a scowl at them both, he stormed out of the door and they heard his footsteps thundering on the stairs.

'I meant every word of it,' Darius said, coming to stand before her. 'I love you. I want to have you with me always. That's why I went to London, to set up the arrangements that would make it possible for me to move here permanently. I suppose I ought to have told you first—*asked* you first—but that's not my way. I fix things to suit myself, and then other people just have to fit in. Once I knew I wanted to marry you, you never had a choice.

'Harriet, Harriet, don't cry. I don't mean it. I'll do anything to marry you. You'll just have to be a little patient with me. Don't cry, my darling, please.'

But she couldn't stop crying. Tears of joy, of hope, of released tension, they all came flooding out, making it impossible for her to speak. Mysteriously, he also found that words had deserted him, so he abandoned them altogether, carried her into the bedroom and revealed his love in other ways. She responded with heartfelt tenderness, and they found that their mutual understanding was once more perfect.

'I can't believe the way you stood up to my father,' he murmured as they lay together afterwards. 'The world is littered with strong men he crushed beneath his feet, but he didn't stand a chance against you.'

'He tried to turn me against you,' she said. 'How dare he!'

'I heard him tell you that he and I had had several meetings while I was in London, but he didn't tell you what those meetings were about. He tried again to get me to marry Freya, offered me money, all useless. Freya was cheering me on, and actually drove me to the airport. The last thing she said to me was, "Go for it. Don't let her escape!"'

'Mary said much the same thing. There'll be a huge cheer when I tell them that we're engaged.' Suddenly, he sounded uncertain. 'Harriet, we are engaged, aren't we?'

'I thought you weren't going to take no for an answer.'

'I'm not.'

'And neither am I.' She drew him close.

'That old man thought he was being clever when he found out about your husband,' Darius said, 'but it just made me angry with him. It only affected me in that I longed for you to confide in me willingly, and when you did—I wanted to tell you that I already knew, but I was afraid to spoil what was happening between us. Say you forgive me.'

'There's nothing to forgive,' she whispered.

'And we'll marry as soon as possible?'

'I want to, of course I do. I love you. I thought I'd never love another man, but you're different from them all. But

can you really give up your old life to come and live here?
Aren't we being unrealistic?'

'I shan't have to give it up completely. I'm going to have
to downsize, but that suits me. My London home is up for
sale and I'll be selling quite a few other properties. I'll pay
off some debts, reschedule others, and what's left can be
controlled just as easily from here as from London.'

'But can you do it all alone?'

'I won't have to. I have staff who are willing to move
here permanently. I couldn't ask them before because I
didn't know where I'd be myself, but now it can all be arranged. I've got plans to create a little village for them.'

'And they won't mind leaving London for such a quiet
place?'

'Mind? They were falling over themselves to volunteer.
This will be a whole new life for a lot of people. It isn't
going to be the "great financial empire" I once had. It'll be
about a third of the size, but that's fine with me. Then I'll
have more time to spend with my wife and our children.'

'Our children?'

'If that's what you'd like.' He was silenced suddenly as
she took him into a fierce embrace.

'That's what I'd like,' she whispered at last. 'Oh, yes,
that's what I'd like, as soon as possible.'

'Then we'll have a dozen children, and I'll spend my
time pottering about the house, and sometimes helping you
in the shop.'

'Now you're getting carried away,' she warned.

'So what's wrong with being carried away?'

'Nothing,' she sighed blissfully. 'Nothing at all.'

'And I'm going to do my best to make Herringdean glad
I'm here. There must be things I can do for the community.
I expect they'll come and suggest them to you soon, and
you can tell me. I'm going to have a good look at that wind

farm. There may be some arrangement I can make to get a good electricity price for the island.'

'Do you really think you can?'

'I don't know.' His voice rose to a note of exhilaration. 'I simply don't know.'

'Darling, you're sounding a bit mad. Anyone would think not knowing was the best thing in the world.'

'Maybe it is. Maybe it's better to have things that you know you don't know, that you've got to learn about, because that's all part of having a new life. There's so much I don't know, and I'm going to have a great time finding out.'

'*We'll* have a great time finding out,' she suggested.

'Maybe. The trouble is that you already know so much more than me. I'm going to have to learn from you—teacher.'

She regarded him tenderly. She wasn't crazy enough to take all of this too seriously. Darius was caught in the exhilaration of their love and their new life, and he was celebrating with wild dreams. But he hadn't completely changed character, no matter how he sounded. Part of him would always be the fierce, dynamic man who'd first arrived on Herringdean weeks ago.

But she knew also that part of him would be this new man coming to life in her arms. And just how the mixture settled would be up to her in the years ahead. He'd put himself in her hands and she was eager for the challenge.

'You make it sound so wonderful,' she said. 'Oh, yes, everything is going to be perfect. No, no, it's perfect now.'

'Not quite,' he said. 'There's still one thing I want, although I don't suppose I'll ever have it.'

'Whatever can that be?'

'You've done so much for me. Saving my life was just the start of it. There are so many other ways in which you've saved me, I couldn't begin to count them. If only there was something I could do for you that would mean as much.'

'But it's enough that you love me.'

'Not for me. I want to give you something so precious that it's like a jewel, but I don't know that I can. I can't make it happen—it just has to happen, and maybe it never will.'

'Stop fretting,' she told him. 'We'll just have to be patient. It may take a long time to happen.'

But it happened before anyone could have expected, and in a way that nobody could have foreseen in a million years.

Preparations for the wedding started at once, with Harriet moving out of her tiny apartment and into Giant's Beacon, where she could take immediate charge of the renovations.

'Is Phantom pleased with his accommodation?' Darius enquired after the first day.

'Yes, he's asked me to express his approval of your efforts on his behalf. Putting him in the room next door to ours was pure genius.'

'Next thing, he'll have to meet the family. We'll start this afternoon.'

'What?'

'It's simple. We go into the computer room, switch on the video link—' he was doing so as he spoke '—and the family will appear.'

It was her first encounter with video link and it took her breath away. Jackson connected from his computer in London, and Marcel appeared from Paris. Then there was Mary and Ken, raising their glasses to her, and Frankie and Mark, bouncing with happiness.

Like Darius, she was discovering the joys of new experiences and they were exhilarating.

'It's all working out,' she told Phantom, stroking him as he settled for the night. 'We're going to have such a wonderful life, my darling—Phantom—are you all right? *Darius.*'

In a moment he was there, dropping to his knees beside the dog, who was heaving violently.

'Call the vet quickly,' he said.

The vet lived nearby. He was soon there, listened to Phantom's heart and shook his head.

'He's very old, and his heart's worn out,' he said. 'This was bound to happen soon. I think you should prepare yourself for the worst. Would you like me to put him to sleep now?'

'No,' Harriet said fiercely. 'I want him until the last possible moment.' She scooped Phantom up in her arms. 'There, darling, we'll stay together and you'll feel my arms around you all the time.'

Darius watched her wretchedly, torn apart by her grief.

'We'll stay with him together,' he said, touching her face gently.

But then the worst thing possible happened. A sound split the air, making them both start up in horror.

'My pager,' she gasped. 'No—no—I can't. I can't leave him to die alone.'

'Harriet, you've got to go,' Darius said urgently. 'Not for their sake but for your own. You swore to do your duty and put it above all personal considerations. If you fail now, you'll never forgive yourself as long as you live.'

Her wild eyes showed that she knew he was right, and tears streamed down her face as she fought between her duty and her feelings for her beloved dog.

'How can I leave him alone?' she whispered.

'He won't be alone. I'll stay with him until the last minute. He'll be in my arms, just as he would have been in yours. He'll know that he's loved, I promise you. Trust me, Harriet. *Trust me!*'

'Yes—' she gasped. 'Yes—' She caressed Phantom's head. 'Goodbye, my darling—goodbye—'

Darius never forgot the look on her face as she backed out of the room. Or the look on Phantom's face as he took the dog into his arms.

'She'd have stayed if she could,' he told him. 'We both know that, because she loves you more than anyone in the world. And I'm not even jealous.'

Incredibly, he felt the great furry body in his arms relax. Phantom's eyes closed, but he was still alive for a moment later they opened again.

'It's time we had a good long talk,' Darius murmured. 'We both love her so much, we had to get together sooner or later.'

He talked on, only faintly aware of the passage of time. He wondered where Harriet was now. Had she reached the station yet? He knew she was suffering, thinking of Phantom dying without her. But he had made her a promise, and he would keep it at all costs.

The hours passed. Daylight faded. He knew he was repeating himself, but that didn't matter. What counted was the love in his voice, reaching out to the dog as Harriet herself would have reached out to him.

At first he listened for her step on the stairs, but gradually he ceased to be aware of anything but the living animal dying softly in his arms. It might be madness but he had no doubt that Phantom could understand every word, just as he would have done from Harriet.

And then the truth came to him as a revelation. This was

the sign he'd longed for, the proof that he and Harriet were one. Phantom's eyes on him were full of trust.

Harriet, slipping into the house downstairs, listened to the silence, knowing what it meant. Phantom had died when she wasn't there to care for him. And however much she tried to believe that Darius had helped him, he would know that she herself had abandoned him when he needed her most. Tears streamed down her face as she climbed the stairs.

And then, halfway up, she stopped, holding herself tense against the incredible sound that reached her. Surely that was Darius's voice? He was talking to someone, that meant—?

Hardly daring to believe it, she sped up the rest of the way, pausing outside the door, then moving quietly into the room. There she stood just outside of Darius's vision, listening, entranced, to his words.

'I'm not sure she really understands even now how much I love her,' he was saying. 'I've tried to show it but I'm clumsy. I never knew anyone like her existed and I'm afraid that she'll leave me. That's why I'm hurrying her into our marriage before she has a chance to think. But she's turning me into someone else. This other guy, he doesn't do any of the things I'm used to, so I'm having to get to know him from scratch.

'I wish I could be more like you. You were never lost for what to do next, were you? Toss them to the ground and jump up and down on them, that's your way.

'I used to be jealous of you. How about that? I thought she loved you because she still loved Brad, but it's got nothing to do with him. I know that now. You're lovable and precious, and you've got to be here for us a while yet.

'Hey, you're restless. That's good. Hold on there, boy.

Don't give up now. She'll be home soon—just a little longer. *Harriet!*'

She dropped down beside him, her hands caressing Phantom, but her eyes turned up to him in a passion of love and gratitude.

'You did it,' she whispered. 'You kept him alive for me. Thank you, thank you—oh, if only you knew—'

'I think perhaps I do,' he murmured, his eyes meeting hers in a moment of total understanding that was normal with them now.

'I reckon he's got a little longer yet,' Darius said.

As if to prove it, Phantom shifted in his arms and leaned forward to lick Harriet's face.

'You've got to live a bit longer, you hear that?' she said. 'I want you there at our wedding. Promise me.'

Woof!

They were married three weeks later, on the beach. Of Darius's family, only Amos and his wife were missing; but his brothers and Freya all said they wouldn't miss it for the world. Mary and Ken said the same thing, watching with satisfaction as Darius laid claim to the most valuable property of his life.

Frankie walked behind the bride, pretty in frills and flowers. And beside her walked Mark, his hand on Phantom's collar, guiding him to a place at the front where he could curl up and watch the ceremony.

The vet had expressed astonishment at his survival, but Harriet wasn't surprised. Darius had done what he longed to do—given her something so precious that it was like a jewel. If she had doubted his love before, she could doubt it no longer. She knew now that the jewel would shine for ever.

* * * * *

Harlequin® Romance

Coming Next Month

Available October 11, 2011

HRCNM0911

REQUEST YOUR FREE BOOKS!
2 FREE NOVELS PLUS 2 FREE GIFTS!

From the Heart, For the Heart

*Harlequin Romantic Suspense presents the latest book
in the scorching new* KELLEY LEGACY *miniseries
from best-loved veteran series author Carla Cassidy*

*Scandal is the name of the game as the Kelley family fights
to preserve their legacy, their hearts...and their lives.*

Read on for an excerpt from the fourth title
RANCHER UNDER COVER

*Available October 2011
from Harlequin Romantic Suspense*

"**W**ould you like a drink?" Caitlin asked as she walked to the minibar in the corner of the room. She felt as if she needed to chug a beer or two for courage.

"No, thanks. I'm not much of a drinking man," he replied.

She raised an eyebrow and looked at him curiously as she poured herself a glass of wine. "A ranch hand who doesn't enjoy a drink? I think maybe that's a first."

He smiled easily. "There was a six-month period in my life when I drank too much. I pulled myself out of the bottom of a bottle a little over seven years ago and I've never looked back."

"That's admirable, to know you have a problem and then fix it."

Those broad shoulders of his moved up and down in an easy shrug. "I don't know how admirable it was, all I knew at the time was that I had a choice to make between living and dying and I decided living was definitely more appealing."

She wanted to ask him what had happened preceding that six-month period that had plunged him into the bottom of the bottle, but she didn't want to know too much about him. Personal information might produce a false sense of intimacy that she didn't need, didn't want in her life.

"Please, sit down," she said, and gestured him to the table. She had never felt so on edge, so awkward in her life.

"After you," he replied.

She was aware of his gaze intensely focused on her as she rounded the table and sat in the chair, and she wanted to tell him to stop looking at her as if she were a delectable dessert he intended to savor later.

Watch Caitlin and Rhett's sensual saga unfold amidst the shocking, ripped-from-the-headlines drama of the Kelley Legacy miniseries in

RANCHER UNDER COVER

Available October 2011 only from Harlequin Romantic Suspense, wherever books are sold.